"I like a man who's honest about his bad intentions."

A corner of Quinn's mouth tugged to the side in something that wasn't quite a grin. Something dangerous, something potent. "If I ever have any of those, I'll be sure to let you know."

"It's a deal."

Quinn lifted a hand to Tess's sweater and ran his fingertips from button to button, along the opening.

"All right, then," he said. And then he grew very still, as only he could do, and looked at Tess in that way that made everything in her aware of everything about him.

Of his height, and his breadth, and his strength, and his ridiculous, impossible appeal.

Dear Reader,

One of my writer's perks is having an excuse to daydream about things that interest me—I can always claim my woolgathering is productive when I weave various elements into the stories I tell. Since one of my interests is building design, I knew that eventually I'd create a character who works as an architect.

Tess Roussel in *A Small-Town Homecoming* is a woman accustomed to seeing her plans followed and her sketches become reality. I had a great time pairing her with Quinn, a man who is determined to build things his way. I'm sure you'll enjoy the fun as this quietly intense hero rocks the self-assured heroine's world to its foundations.

I'd love to hear from my readers! Please come for a visit to my Web site at www.terrymclaughlin.com, or find me at www.wetnoodleposse.com or www.superauthors.com, or write to me at P.O. Box 5838, Eureka, CA 95502.

Wishing you happily-ever-after reading,

Terry McLaughlin

A SMALL-TOWN HOMECOMING
Terry McLaughlin

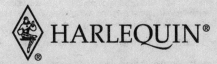

TORONTO • NEW YORK • LONDON
AMSTERDAM • PARIS • SYDNEY • HAMBURG
STOCKHOLM • ATHENS • TOKYO • MILAN • MADRID
PRAGUE • WARSAW • BUDAPEST • AUCKLAND

Recycling programs
for this product may
not exist in your area.

ISBN-13: 978-0-373-71566-4

A SMALL-TOWN HOMECOMING

Copyright © 2009 by Teresa A. McLaughlin.

This edition published by arrangement with Harlequin Books S.A.

® and TM are trademarks of the publisher. Trademarks indicated with
® are registered in the United States Patent and Trademark Office, the
Canadian Trade Marks Office and in other countries.

www.eHarlequin.com

Printed in U.S.A.

ABOUT THE AUTHOR

Terry McLaughlin spent a dozen years teaching a variety of subjects, including anthropology, music appreciation, English, drafting, drama and history, to a variety of students from kindergarten to college before she discovered romance novels and fell in love with love stories. When she's not reading or writing, she enjoys traveling and planning house and garden improvement projects. Terry lives with her husband in Northern California on a tiny ranch in the redwoods. Visit her at www.terrymclaughlin.com.

Books by Terry McLaughlin

HARLEQUIN SUPERROMANCE

1348–LEARNING CURVE
1372–MAKE-BELIEVE COWBOY*
1400–THE RANCHER NEEDS A WIFE*
1438–MAYBE, BABY*
1467–A PERFECT STRANGER
1488–A SMALL-TOWN TEMPTATION**

*Bright Lights, Big Sky
**Built to Last

For the baristas at Gold Rush, who help keep me going with smiles and Cold Snap Mochas.

CHAPTER ONE

TESS ROUSSEL sidled through her Main Street office doorway a quarter of an hour past the posted opening time. She maneuvered a stylish leather briefcase, two rolled elevation plans, an oversize clutch purse, a custard-filled maple bar and her triple-butterscotch latte past the jamb, but coffee slopped through the cup lid and splattered over her gray suede heels.

"Not again." She inhaled April air smelling of last night's special at the trattoria across the street and this morning's catch on the docks two blocks over. And then she blew it out with a disgusted sigh. "Damn parking meters."

Shoving the door closed with her hip, she flipped a row of light switches with an elbow. It wasn't that she was too cheap to spend her work breaks feeding coins into one of the meters stationed along Main Street, although the daily expense competed with the cost of her favorite caffeinated beverages. And it wasn't that she was too forgetful to deal with the meters' payment schedule, especially after four parking tickets had forced her to devise an alarm system that could penetrate her deepest levels of concentration and summon her from her design work.

It was the principle of the thing. Potential customers

shouldn't have to pay for the privilege of popping into the Victorian-era storefronts crowding Carnelian Cove's marina district. And the merchants shouldn't have to pay for the convenience of parking near their own places of business. And she shouldn't have to make the hike from the stingy public lot three long blocks down the street. And definitely not twice on such a drizzly morning, just because she had too much stuff to tote safely in one load. And not in these heels.

Although the shoes attached to the heels were simply fabulous.

Her stylish heels clicked across the scarred plank floor, echoing in the high-ceilinged space. Usually she enjoyed the ambience of her one-of-a-kind office—the subtle industrial spotlights punctuating the softer illumination of period fanlights, the brick side walls separating her office from the used bookstore on one side and the gardening boutique on the other, the touches of sharp black lines and bright red paint and delicate greenery. But this morning, in the fog-dimmed daylight trickling through the street-front bay windows, everything looked a little worn-out and washed-up.

Kind of like the way she'd be feeling if she let herself dwell too long on her problems. She dumped the briefcase, purse and elevations on her drafting table and scowled at today's project: a contractor's rough sketch for a bowling alley renovation she'd agreed to transform into a permit-ready plan. Not exactly the glamorous career she'd envisioned while slaving through her university design classes. And nothing like the exciting projects she'd worked on during her seven years with one of San Francisco's most prestigious architectural firms.

Her father, a dashing, aristocratic Frenchman whose

work had dazzled the city's art connoisseurs before his untimely death, would have shuddered at the bourgeois assignment. Her mother, owner of the Bay area's finest art gallery, would probably cringe at the dull practicality of the finish details.

But drawing restroom updates and adding more diner space to Cove Lanes was the only kind of work available in this compact northern California town on the Pacific coast. She knew she should be grateful for the crumbs the local contractors had tossed her way since she'd arrived a year ago, though she understood why they were so quick to give her this particular share of their business: builders wanted to build, not fuss over paperwork.

Yes, she understood—more than any of them realized. As much as she enjoyed the process of design, of crafting neat, two-dimensional schemes that would be transformed into three-dimensional works of art, it was nothing compared to the thrill of helping to shape her creation on the job site. The buzz and clang of equipment, the smell of sawdust and solvents, the skeleton and organs and nerves and skin of studs and plumbing and wiring and siding—every step was fascinating and exciting and *hers*. Every detail and decision was hers to choose and make, and the sense of power and control was addictive. Every line and corner and arc sprang from her imagination, and watching it all rise from the ground was a rush beyond compare.

She switched on her music system and selected her favorite Miles Davis album—something cool to match the day, a bluesy tune to match her mood. No one in Carnelian Cove considered hiring an architect when there were plenty of contractors willing to secure a building permit with the inexpensive—and unimaginative—

basics. That's how things had always been done, and most people couldn't see a reason to do things differently. She'd known it might take a while to change their minds, and she'd been prepared to watch her savings dwindle during the adjustment period. But she hadn't realized there might never be any genuine design business for her architecture firm.

Her very own firm, her long-time dream: Roussel Designs. She sighed and carried her maple bar and her cooling latte across her office to study the model occupying the prime real estate in the windows fronting Main Street: the model for Tidewaters. Retail spaces for six smart boutiques and offices, a midsize restaurant at dock level and five spacious multilevel condominiums above. A wonderful boardwalk fronting the bay and an open, parklike space surrounding the parking area— ample, meter-free parking. A harmonious blend of commercial use and stylish housing, a contemporary building reflecting local traditions, an ideal example for future waterfront redevelopment.

And it was absolutely, positively *gorgeous.*

She bit into her pastry and licked creamy custard from the corner of her mouth. She'd get Tidewaters built, all right. She'd pull it from her imagination and raise it from the ground, and then they'd see the three-dimensional proof of what she had inside her. She'd show them all what she could do—everyone back in San Francisco who'd warned her she'd never make it on her own, everyone here in the Cove who didn't think an architect could make a difference, everyone in her family who'd patronized her ambitions and doubted her abilities.

Everyone but her grandmother, Geneva Chandler. Grandmère didn't need proof of her granddaughter's talent and determination. She'd already put up the financial backing for the construction and had been calling in her political markers for this building she wanted as much as Tess did herself. They'd make a hell of a team.

Tess shifted her shoulders, uncomfortable with the possibility of comparisons to Geneva Chandler. She loved the old woman, but her grandmother could be powerfully intimidating.

A streak of sunlight pierced the low-lying fog along the bay, and the interior of Tess's office brightened. The fog would clear by midmorning, and another gorgeous spring day would lift her spirits. Good weather for building something.

And time to get started on the day's work.

She turned to face her desk, ready to draw the bowling alley plans on her computer's CAD system, and saw her answering machine's red eye blinking from beneath a messy stack of bills. The display listed the number for Chandler House.

"Tess, dear," scolded Geneva's recorded voice. "You're late."

"I know." Tess snatched at the bills before they toppled over the edge of the desk.

"If you're going to advertise office hours, you must make more of an effort to keep them," the machine continued. "It's part of a polished professional appearance."

"Get to the point," Tess muttered.

"But that's not why I called." Grandmère paused for dramatic effect. "I want you to cancel your morning appointments—"

"As if I had any," Tess said with a sigh.

"—and meet me here, at Chandler House. I'll expect you by eleven. No later than eleven," Grandmère emphasized. "You can practice your punctuality on one of your relatives, who manages to love you in spite of your shortcomings."

Tidewaters. She had news—that had to be the reason for this summons. Tess pressed a hand to her jittery stomach and sank into her desk chair.

A city council meeting was scheduled for tonight, and the waterfront zoning issue was on the agenda. Again. Grandmère had been pulling strings behind the scenes, postponing a vote until she was sure the results would go her way. She still carried plenty of political clout in this town, and several of the council members already agreed with her plans.

They were right to agree—Tidewaters would be a genuine asset to the city. It would develop a weed-choked gap along the waterfront, provide new jobs and help reinvigorate the quaint, older business section of town—and all on someone else's dime. Tess had been astounded that anyone would refuse Geneva Chandler's offer to build such a wonderful, beautiful place in the heart of her community. But the opposition to development had been fierce. There were many here who wished things to remain as they were, who viewed progress with suspicion and the land at water's edge as untouchable.

Tess set the remains of the maple bar aside, wiped her sticky fingers and tried to concentrate on her work. But she couldn't shake the case of nerves or the unsettling swings from elation to dread that kept her stomach churning. Even if her grandmother had won this battle, even if construction were about to begin, Tess wondered if the war over the waterfront would quietly move underground.

And she didn't like the idea of building on such a shaky foundation.

PRECISELY one hour later, Tess drove her roadster up the long, winding approach to Chandler House. Early shrub roses edged the drive, and puffs of cotton-candy blooms dotted the rhododendron bushes spreading beneath the lacy canopy of a redwood grove. With each bend in the road, she caught a glimpse of the creamy yellow shingle-style mansion rising at the edge of Whaler's Bluff.

Her great-grandfather, an ambitious man who rose from lumberjack to mill owner, had purchased the site and planned for a great house overlooking the growing town. His son, a clever man who launched several local businesses and invested in others, created that house to showcase the family's wealth. Both men had used their money—and that of the heiresses they married—to benefit Carnelian Cove and their own positions in the community. Both had filled various city political offices; both had served as mayor.

Tess's mother had spent her childhood in the fairy-tale house, her room overlooking the crescent-shaped sprawl of Carnelian Cove. The building's fanciful bays and jutting windows, its wide porches and shadowed niches had filled Tess's imagination with romantic scenes during the holidays and summers she'd spent here as a girl, and she wondered—as she so often did lately—whether this grand old place was the source of her fascination with architecture.

She slowed as she passed through the gap in an imposing black iron gate, admiring the stone steps that marched from the leaded-glass entry to meet the dramatic sweep of pristine lawn. Pale green ferns spilled from wicker stands, and the porch swing sported bright new pillows striped in sherbet shades. One of Grandmère's fussy, yappy little terriers dashed to the top of the steps and sounded the alarm.

Though she'd have preferred to continue to the rear service area and enter through the modest kitchen door, Tess pulled beneath the stately porte cochere shading the side entrance. She was a grown woman now—and gathering every one of her thirty-one years about her like a shield. She didn't need the additional fortification of a cookie stolen from Julia's fat jar to help her face her formidable grandmother. But she did take a moment to run a comb through her hair and freshen her lipstick before she stepped from her car. Geneva Chandler wasn't simply Grandmère this afternoon—she was a business associate.

The heavy oak door opened and two more yipping, beribboned dogs escaped to circle Tess's car. Geneva stood in the doorway, a tall woman whose regal stance was softened by pink cashmere, pearls and a welcoming smile. "Right on time," she said.

"I can manage when it matters." Tess grinned and waded through the pack of terriers sniffing at her ankles. "And I was hoping you might reward me with lunch."

"I might at that, if you don't mind sharing a plate of cheese and fruit." Geneva wrapped her in a quick, tight hug that smelled of Chanel and felt like summer. "Julia has the afternoon off."

If Julia had prepared the plate before she'd left for the day, the cheese would be brie and the fruit would be fresh and arranged with artistic flair. Grandmère's cook may have rapped Tess's fingers with a wooden spoon more than once when they'd inched toward the cake frosting or strayed into the sugar bowl, but she'd always found time for a kitchen visit, inviting Tess to perch on

one of the tall stools around the gigantic island, oohing
and aahing over the news of the day while she stirred
the makings of something fabulous in one of her huge
crockery pots.

"Sounds like you might be needing some company,"
Tess said as she stepped into the cool side hall.

"Depends on the company."

"I could manage to be on my best behavior."

"Don't beg, Tess, dear," Geneva said with a shiver.
"It's so…unnerving."

Tess laughed and bent to scoop one of the terriers into
the crook of her arm and then grimaced as a quick pink
tongue scored a direct hit on her lower lip. "Ugh."

"You're getting slow in your old age." Geneva turned
and headed down the narrow servants' passage. "Please
wipe your mouth and join me in my office."

Tess set down the dog, tightened her fingers around
her purse and followed her grandmother. A summons to
the office had rarely ended well. Grandmère had always
favored that spot for issuing difficult requests or doling
out punishments.

Her grandmother ushered her into the small, thickly
paneled room and then pulled the tall pocket door closed
on its silent track. Tess's heels sank into the thick
Aubusson carpet, and she inhaled the familiar scents of
old books and furniture oil. Sunlight shot through the
ruby reds and cobalt blues of the stained-glass panes above
the lace curtains and pinned rainbows on the portraits of
Chandlers in military uniforms and Victorian gowns. The
spired mantel clock, wedged between a pair of smudge-
snouted Staffordshire spaniels, ticked away the seconds.

"Have a seat, Tess." Geneva crossed to a cabinet.
"This won't take long."

Tess perched on the edge of one of the delicate chairs near Geneva's desk. Neatly stacked on the desk's surface were correspondence and newsletters, no doubt from the Historical Society, the Garden Club, the Ladies' League, the University Foundation Committee. As one of the Cove's leading citizens, Geneva liked to keep a finger in every social pie in the county.

"I know it's a bit early for this," she said as she dribbled sherry into two dainty goblets, "but I think we can indulge ourselves just this once."

Tess hesitated before taking the glass. She rarely drank—her mother had done enough of that for everyone in the family. She stared at the golden liquid in the elaborately etched crystal and told herself there was no harm in it, just this once. She sipped and braced for the burn along her throat, and then she lowered the drink to her lap and waited for her grandmother to explain the reason for her summons.

"I spoke with Arlie Ratliff again today." Geneva settled in one of the high-backed chairs flanking the fireplace and regarded Tess over the rim of her glass. "He's had a change of heart."

Tess clutched the arm of her chair. The city councilman had been on the fence about changing the zoning of Geneva's waterfront property to allow for commercial development. "Would this change have anything to do with Tidewaters?"

"Yes. He assures me he'll vote for rezoning at tonight's council meeting."

"And we'll have the building permit in hand by tomorrow afternoon." Elated, Tess raised her glass in a toast. "You did it."

"Arlie owed me a favor or two." Geneva swirled the sherry in her glass with a sly smile. "I simply had to jog his memory a bit. And then promise him I'd forget all about it myself."

Tess held up a hand. "Whatever it was, I don't want to hear it."

"Are you sure?" Geneva's smile widened. "It would make for some excellent lunch conversation before it gets wiped from my memory for good."

"Geneva Chandler, you can be one hell of a scary lady."

"Thank you, dear."

Tess rose and paced the room, unable to sit still. "I can't believe it. Tidewaters—it's actually going to happen. I'm going to build it."

"Yes." Geneva lowered her glass to the piecrust table beside her chair. "In a manner of speaking."

"It's going to be gorgeous. Fabulous."

"Tess…"

"I know you've seen the model often enough—and I did a fabulous job on that, too, if I do say so myself, but—"

"*Tess*." Geneva raised a hand. "Please. Sit down."

Something in the tone of her grandmother's voice had Tess's stomach jackknifing to her knees. "What is it?" she asked as she sank back into her chair.

"It's about the contractor I've chosen for the project."

"You've chosen—" Tess took a deep breath, slamming a lid on her temper and her anxiety. "You promised to consult with me on that. I explained how important it was to find someone who could work with me to implement my vision. *Our* vision."

"Well, yes, I did. But that was before my meeting with Arlie."

"I see." Tess set her glass on the desk. "Someone else helped him change his mind."

"It's not what you're thinking." Geneva twisted her fingers through her pearls.

"You couldn't possibly know what I'm thinking." *Or what I'm feeling.* Tess sucked in another long breath and ordered herself, again, to stay calm. "This is someone I'll be working with so closely it'll be as if we're the same person. Someone who'll have to practically read my mind and help fashion what's inside me."

"I'm sure you two will figure things out as you go."

Tess narrowed her eyes. "Who is it?"

"Quinn."

"Quinn." The name was like a physical blow.

"Arlie says he's very good."

"He wasn't so good a few years ago." Quinn had skipped town after an accident on a job site had put one of his crew in the hospital. "And he's an alcoholic."

"Recovered."

Tess knew all about "recovered" alcoholics. Those in her experience had never managed to stay recovered for long, no matter how much the people who loved them might beg. She rose from her seat to prowl around the room, swamped with ghostlike reactions, trapped in a never-ending loop of helplessness and resentment, tempted to gnaw a fingernail as she used to. But the moment she'd raise her hand toward her mouth, Grandmère would click her tongue and shake her head. That, too, was part of the old patterns.

Geneva picked up her sherry and took another sip. "I'm convinced Quinn's the right man for the job."

"Because you have so much experience with this sort of thing."

"Because I have a great deal of experience reading people, yes." The woman in pastel pink straightened her spine and leveled a severe look at Tess. "Quinn has assured me he can complete this job on time and on budget. And I believe him."

"You've met with him?" A dull pain layered over the shock of betrayal. Her grandmother had done this without consulting her, knowing how much this project meant to her. Knowing how many dreams she'd poured into her sketches and plans.

"Yes."

"I see." Tess stared out the window, watching the waves beating against the rocks. "It's decided, then."

"I've offered him the contract. I expect his answer by the end of the day."

"I'm sure you'll get the answer you want." A job this size would provide steady employment through the entire building season—and plenty of corners to cut to pad the contractor's profit.

She turned to face her tough-as-nails grandmother. "You always do, Mémère."

CHAPTER TWO

QUINN SLUMPED against the toolbox wedged in one side of his pickup bed, legs hanging over the edge of the open tailgate, and scanned three acres of weed-covered ground studded with refuse. From the cracked curb on the Front Street boundary to the gap-toothed riprap edging the foot of a disintegrating dock, the ground rose and fell in random, jagged waves.

Tomorrow he'd haul in an office trailer and set up shop. In one week, he'd have this place scraped clean and the footings ready to dig. By the end of the month he'd have gravel spread and neat piles of form boards and rebar placed and ready for the foundation work. And before the end of the year he'd be putting the finishing details on the finest building Carnelian Cove had seen erected in over fifty years.

He inhaled deeply, enjoying the cool blend of trampled Scotch broom, sea-salted air and the rich tang of tobacco smoke from the cigarette dangling between his fingers. And then he braced while a sharp-taloned need clawed its way through him. His personal battle with his alcohol addiction was a day-by-day siege, but nothing was proving as difficult as trying to deny his craving for tobacco.

Denial—a daily exercise and a constant companion of late. The tamped-down disappointments and regrets, the low-grade itching and yearning for something—for anything—better than what he had, colored his existence and kept him moving in the right direction. That and the daughter waiting for him at home.

Rosie wanted him to quit smoking, and he'd do it for her. He'd do anything for her—anything within reason. She needed that from him right now, needed his reassurance as much as his steadiness. She'd lost so much lately—hell, she'd lost just about everything she had to lose during her short life. He had so much to make up to her.

He studied the thin stream of smoke curling from the cigarette. Rosie had been five when his drinking had driven his ex-wife away, and Nancy had taken their daughter with her to Oregon. He'd never forget the way Rosie had clung to his pant leg that last night, sobbing, promising to be good, promising to remember to feed her turtle if only she could stay in her room, stay in her new school with her new friends. Begging him to come with them when it was time to go.

He'd promised to feed her turtle for her. But he'd been too wrapped up in his own misery, too drunk to remember, and he'd let her pet die. His daughter's dry-eyed acceptance of this betrayal had been the turning point. He hadn't had a drink since the turtle's funeral.

Now Rosie's mom had a new man in her life, a guy who didn't want a ten-year-old cramping his style. And since his ex had never been the kind of woman who could function for long without a man, she'd sent her daughter packing, back to her father. Just for a while, Nancy had told him, just until this new relationship settled into something permanent. In the meantime, it was Quinn's turn to deal with Rosie.

So he'd deal.

He'd had her four months now. Four long, difficult months of figuring out a new routine, of learning how to balance the long hours on the job with the responsibilities of a full-time parent. Of watching Rosie struggling with another start in a new school and the uncertain business of making new friends. Trying to deal with him.

Four long months to decide he wanted his own new relationship to be permanent, too. He was going to keep Rosie here, with him.

He sighed and fingered the cigarette in his hand, fighting the urge to raise it to his lips for just one puff, and then a streak of scarlet roared past and slowed near the end of the block. He narrowed his eyes as a familiar BMW Z4 roadster bumped over the gap in the curb at the entrance to the construction site and edged onto a patch of rough gravel.

Tess Roussel, architect. The nominal head of this project, though they both knew she couldn't make a move without him.

The driver-side door swung open and one long, slim, short-skirted leg stretched toward the ground. *Nice.* Too bad it was attached at the hip to a harpy with an agenda.

She rose, slowly, and slammed the door behind her, pausing to glare at him across the ruins. He knew her eyes were the color of bourbon and every bit as seductive, that her scent could make his mouth water and send his system into overdrive. And the fact that he'd wanted her the moment he'd set eyes on her didn't mean spit. He'd been controlling far more serious thirsts for years.

She strode toward him on her ridiculous shoes, risking injury to one of her shapely ankles with every wobble of those skyscraper heels. The breeze off the bay tossed her short black hair across her forehead, and she lifted an elegant, long-fingered hand to brush it back into place. She wore a no-nonsense gray suit, the kind of suit a woman wore when she wanted to look like a man. The kind of suit that clung to lush, womanly curves and accentuated the fact that she was a female.

She halted in front of him and raised one of her perfectly arched brows. "Quinn."

"Roussel."

She lowered her gaze to his cigarette and slowly lifted it again to meet his. "Smoking on the job site?" she asked.

He brought the cigarette to his lips just to watch those whiskey-colored eyes darken with displeasure. "Against the rules?"

"Are you asking for a clarification?"

"Figured that's why you're here." He squinted at her through the smoke. "To set things straight," he said.

"Plenty of time for that later." She slipped her hands into her jacket pockets and turned toward the bay. "It's a great site."

"Best in town."

"It will be."

She angled her face in his direction, waiting for him to comment, but he simply met and held her stare.

God, she was a looker. He'd mostly seen her in passing, striding down Main Street as if she owned the strip, or crossing those long legs on a tall stool at one of the waterfront bars. And he'd noticed the way men's gazes followed her, tracked her, undressed her, coveted her. A real heartbreaker. A real ball-buster, too. The kind of woman who enjoyed the attention, as long as it was on her terms.

He'd never had the chance to study her like this, up close. Right now, with the sun sinking over her shoulder and setting the highlights in her hair aflame, with her sculpted chin tipped up in challenge and those thick, sooty lashes drifting low over her wide-set eyes, she was even more of a looker than he'd realized.

Her gaze settled on the six-pack nestled in a rope coil on the truck bed behind him, and her glossy red lips thinned in disapproval.

Beer for the crew, a small celebration for the big job ahead. She needn't worry—he had no intention of joining them in the drinking part of the festivities. Not that it was any of her business. "Something bothering you?" he asked.

"Yeah." She shifted her stance and narrowed her eyes. "Plenty."

"Same goes."

"Oh, I doubt that." Her mouth turned up at the corners in a catlike smile. "I don't think it's the same kind of bother at all."

He slid to the ground and moved in close, close enough to note the slight flutter of her lashes and hear the sharp and sudden intake of her breath. His blood heated with something more than the basic tension between them. In her heels, she was nearly eye to eye with him, and he wondered how she'd fit alongside him if he snaked an arm around her narrow waist and hauled her to him. "No harm in a little creative thinking," he said.

"Is that so?"

He dropped his gaze to her mouth, testing her. Testing himself. He wanted this job, damn it. He'd just signed a contract saying he'd take it on. He wanted to earn a chunk of money so he wouldn't have to worry about his ex's first legal maneuver in the inevitable custody war. He wanted his daughter to be proud of the work he was doing, even if that work was going to mean long hours away from home, away from her. The last thing he needed was another battle on his hands with another woman who could pile on the guilt of his past failures.

A woman who could give him one more thing to crave.

He looked Tess straight in the eye. "Yeah."

"All right, then." She turned to go, tossing a wicked smile over her shoulder. "See you around, Quinn."

He dropped the cigarette and crushed it into the ground. "I'll be here."

LATER THAT EVENING, after she'd changed into her most comfortable jeans, her softest designer loafers and dined on a frisée salad with her special raspberry vinaigrette dressing, Tess drove toward Driftwood. The residential area south of the town center offered a certain rustic charm, particularly where the streetlights thinned and the pavement faded to crunchy gravel roads, where lacy-branched redwoods crowded the shoreline and cast their long shadows over wave-splashed rocks. The neighborhoods she passed wore a jumble of styles, and the houses perching in the open spaces among the trees often reflected the personalities of their owners rather than the period of their construction.

Normally Tess enjoyed a trip through Driftwood at this time of night, when the amber glow of early-evening lamplight provided glimpses of prairie-style mantelpieces, paneled doors, arching doorways and coved ceilings before the home owners drew their curtains to shut out the dark. She might have enjoyed restoring one of the vintage houses in this part of town, but she'd found a place that suited her along the river, a more practical house that wouldn't require messy repairs or put a dent in her budget making them.

Tonight she wasn't in the mood to notice much more than the widening pothole on Daylily Lane and her own negative attitude. Her chat with Quinn had siphoned most of the joy from what was supposed to be the first triumph of her professional career.

All she'd wanted was some time alone on the site to look at the place and to know—to truly believe—that what was in her imagination was actually, finally going to appear. A few minutes to let her imagination loose, to fill that space with all the possibilities she held inside. Her very own creation, her very own miracle—hers and hers alone, for the first and last time.

Only it hadn't been hers, because she hadn't been alone. She'd been forced to share it with Quinn. Just as she would be forced to share every step of its creation with him for the next nine months, to maintain her vision through his interpretation and consult with him on its progress. To share the end result, too: her design, his construction.

Quinn Construction. She tightened her grip on the steering wheel. He had a lot riding on this project, too. He was rehabbing his professional reputation as well as his personal life. If he pulled off this job—the largest in the Cove at the moment—without a hitch, he'd be well on his way to establishing himself as a competent builder, not to mention banking a sizable profit.

And in order to maximize that profit, he'd want to complete the job as quickly and as cheaply as possible. Which meant they'd argue over the specs. Contractors always tried to shave their costs by changing the specs—after they'd used those same specs to draw up their bids for the project in the first place. She wanted Tidewaters to be spectacular; he'd want it to be finished.

If only he weren't so…so…so damned *attractive*. Those craggy, lived-in looks, that haunted, stoic air. Thick black hair layered in unruly waves, sensuous lips above a dented chin. *Yum*. Even the intense gaze he aimed at her with those shockingly blue, deep-set eyes could send tiny shivers skittering up her spine at the same time it ratcheted up her annoyance. She'd always been a sucker for a bad boy, and Quinn was as bad as they came.

Beyond bad. A disaster, considering his problem with drinking and her problem with drinkers.

Besides, lusting after a business partner couldn't be good for a working relationship, especially one that was so important to them both. Especially when that relationship threatened to be antagonistic. Although *she* didn't intend to be antagonistic…not at first, anyway. She'd be generous and let him make the first wrong move.

Smiling grimly in anticipation of the coming battles, she pulled into the narrow gravel drive beside Charlie Keene's tiny bungalow and plucked a dog biscuit from the box tucked behind her seat. Then she climbed from her car, lifting a pink bakery bag high above her head.

"Down," she ordered the black Labrador retriever streaking across the shadowy yard. "Stay down, or you won't get your bribe, you fur-faced shakedown artist."

Charlie's obnoxious pet rammed its wide black nose into her crotch before she could toss the biscuit across the yard. "Good riddance," she muttered as the dog raced after it, and then she glanced at the muddy paw prints on her shoes with a sigh. At least the monster hadn't left a matching set on her jeans and jacket.

Charlie's fiancé, Jack Maguire, must have been making some progress with the obedience training.

He'd certainly made some progress with Charlie's house. As Tess strode up the narrow path toward her friend's freshly painted forest-green front door, she noted the neatly clipped lawn and the new willow tree staked in one corner of the yard. Charlie hadn't done much more than dump her junk in the place after she'd bought it last year, but Jack was slowly and surely turning the fixer-upper into a charming home they'd share after their wedding. Charlie had always needed a keeper, and in Jack she'd found a man who liked to keep things the way they ought to be kept.

Actually, it had been Jack who'd found Charlie. He'd arrived in the Cove nearly three months ago, investigating the area's sand and gravel supply for his employer. Within two weeks of checking out the local situation—and meeting Charlie—he'd quit his job, made an offer to buy out her competition and slyly cornered her with a deal she couldn't refuse: combining their two ready mix companies with a wedding. At first she'd fought him with every weapon in her arsenal, but in the end she'd agreed to a mutually beneficial business arrangement and accepted his marriage proposal.

For a man whose words tended to ramble along in a syrupy drawl, Jack Maguire could do some fast talking when it suited him.

Tess lifted the period knocker and let it fall against the hammered plate, pleased with the solid *thwump* of the heavy iron. The man had taste. He also had an ego the size of the Pacific, but at least that Southern-fried charm of his helped soften the most outrageous excesses.

More than she could say for the prickly contractor she'd had to deal with before dinner. Nothing soft or charming there.

Charlie opened the door. "Thought you'd never get here," she said as she snatched the bag from Tess's hands and tugged her inside. "Addie brought a stack of bridal magazines, and she's making me look at pictures again. Tell her to stop, or I'm going to shoot you both right now and eat all the cookies myself."

Tess tossed her jacket over the arm of a club chair and settled beside their friend, Addie Sutton, on the plump sofa. Addie owned a stained-glass shop a block from Tess's office, where she was creating some fabulous windows for Tidewaters. She had more artistic talent in her dainty fingers than Tess had in her entire body, and yet Tess loved her in spite of it. Everyone loved Addie, in the same way everyone loved puppies and pizza. It was inevitable.

"Where's Jack?" Tess asked. "I brought one of Marie-Claudette's cookies just for him. One shaped like a big, fat mouth."

"Baseball practice." Addie turned a thick, glossy magazine in Tess's direction and pointed to a photo of a model buried in clouds of white tulle and baby's breath. "Isn't this gorgeous?"

"Yeah, if you've got something to hide—like the bride and half the wedding party."

Leave it to Addie, who could pass for a French bisque doll with her spun-gold hair and long-lashed eyes, to go for the ruffles. But anyone who knew Charlie knew she was allergic to frills. Tess took the magazine and flipped through more pages, looking for something sleek and simple. A classic gown with a touch of pizzazz or a hint of drama, just to keep things interesting. "Do we have a date yet? Or a venue?"

Charlie shrugged. "I'm working on it."

"That's what you said last week." Tess paused to admire a striking bouquet of calla lilies. "You mustn't be working very hard."

"Don't nag."

"Don't worry. I figure Maudie and Ben are double-teaming you on a daily basis." Charlie's mother, Maudie, had recently announced her own engagement to Ben Chandler, Geneva's relation by marriage and a distant cousin of Tess's. But Maudie had made it clear she wouldn't begin planning for her own wedding until she'd seen her daughter walk down the aisle.

Tess turned the page and sighed over a picture of a dark-haired bride in an elegant sheath with a plunging back. "How about this?"

Addie craned her neck to study the shot. "It would look great…on you."

"Yes, it would. Too bad I'm not in the market right now." She closed the magazine with a sigh and slumped against the cushions. "I've got news."

Charlie leaned a shoulder against the arched entry to her dining room. "Champagne news or beer news?"

"Beer doesn't go with cookies." Addie wrinkled her turned-up nose in disgust.

"Neither does champagne," Tess said, "but hey, don't let that stop us. If you've got any," she added.

"*Please.*" Charlie grinned. "Jack would be insulted to hear you question the quality of his wine cellar."

"Jack's not here." Tess raised one eyebrow. "And since when did he start missing out on an evening with you?"

"Since he got sucked into his own plot to prove his

community spirit and volunteered to coach Little League." Charlie straightened and headed toward the kitchen. "I'll go get the party plastic and be right back."

"What are we celebrating?" Addie tucked a long blond curl behind one ear. "Is this about your waterfront project? About the windows?"

Addie's shop forever teetered on the brink of bankruptcy, but that wasn't the only reason Tess had incorporated touches of stained glass in her design. They added a vintage detail that would help the building blend with its Victorian-era neighbors.

Charlie walked into the room carrying a bottle and a small stack of plastic cups and paper napkins. "I hear Quinn got the job."

"So much for my big news."

Charlie shrugged. "Small town."

"Big mouths." Tess took the napkins and fanned them across the coffee table. "Bigger noses. I don't know why *The Cove Press* bothers competing."

"Isn't Quinn the contractor who left town a few years ago?" asked Addie. "Something about an accident on a job site?"

"Yeah." Tess sighed dramatically. "But he's back."

"Heard his wife left him." Addie frowned. "Heard he had a drinking problem, too."

"*Had* being the important word here." Charlie popped the cork from the bottle. "Jack likes him."

"Jack likes everyone," Tess pointed out. "He's been seen buying crushed cans from the crazy guy who sells trash down by the wharf. He even continued to like you while you were trying to run him out of town a couple of months ago."

"You shouldn't lump Charlie in the same sentence

with Crazy Ed." Addie folded back a page in the magazine on her lap and passed it to Tess. "How about this gown? The lace is so delicate."

"You shouldn't lump Charlie in the same sentence as *delicate*," Tess said, handing back the magazine.

"Don't bother showing me," Charlie mumbled around a mouthful of sugar cookie. "I'm only the bride."

Tess watched her soon-to-be-married friend stack her booted heels on the rickety coffee table. The tomboyish redhead would be horrified to hear that her pint-size frame and pixie-style nose were two of the most obvious items on a long list of features that could be termed *delicate*.

"Isn't Quinn the guy who drives that big black truck?" asked Addie. "The one with the gold shamrock on the door?"

"That's him." Tess scowled. "He was at the site tonight when I swung by to gloat. Spoiled a perfectly good mood."

"Which happens so rarely." Addie shot her a sideways glance. "He's kind of…"

Tess narrowed her eyes. "Kind of what?"

"Kind of…hot."

"Hot?"

"*Hot*," Charlie said. "H-O-T. Not that I'd notice, being engaged to someone who's even hotter."

"Hot. Huh." Tess shrugged to prove her disinterest, even if she agreed with her friends. "I suppose. If you go for tall, dark and brooding."

"Who doesn't?" Addie shared a knowing grin with Charlie. "Especially you, Tess."

"Brooding gets old after a while." Tess straightened with a sigh. "I know I'm getting tired of it myself, tonight. Time for some fun. Time to pick out a dress."

"And flowers," Addie said.

Charlie groaned and slumped in her chair. "I thought this was supposed to be a party in honor of Tess's big news."

"It is." Tess poured a half inch of champagne into her cup. "And this is how I want to celebrate."

"By making me miserable?"

"You know what they say about misery," Tess said. "It loves company."

"Thanks a lot," muttered Charlie.

"Any time." Tess grabbed a sugar cookie and snuggled back against the sofa cushions. "What are friends for?"

CHAPTER THREE

QUINN EDGED his way through his apartment door that night with his arms full of breakfast supplies and a fast-food dinner. "Hi, Neva."

"Here, let me take that." Neva Yergin, his elderly neighbor and part-time sitter, shuffled toward him to take one of the sacks and set it on the narrow counter in his tiny kitchen. "You're back earlier than I expected."

"Hope I didn't interrupt *Trivia Maze*."

She shook her head. "Commercial break. But I'd better scoot next door before they start round two."

"Okay." He pulled the quart of milk and canned cat food she'd asked him to pick up for her from one of the sacks and set them aside. "How's that disposal working?"

"Like a charm. Thanks again for fixing it."

"No problem."

Neva slipped her things into her bulging tote and headed toward the door. "She got home right on time. Been sitting at that computer all afternoon."

Quinn stopped short of a sigh. He didn't approve of Rosie's method for shutting herself away, but he couldn't ask Neva to drag his daughter out of her room and force her to find something better to do with her time. His neighbor was doing far too much for him already, more than he could repay with the rent he subsidized, or the occasional repair or sack of groceries.

"Thanks, Neva," he said as the door closed behind her.

He moved into the cramped space that served as a combination living and dining room and switched off the television. The radiator rattled and wheezed and coughed up traces of mildew and aging plaster. Beyond the tall, grime-streaked window overlooking Third Street, a siren's wail competed with the hum of passing traffic. Not the best place for raising a kid, but he'd had his own needs in mind when he'd signed the lease for an efficiency apartment two floors above the Karapoulis Travel Agency storefront.

And if they moved away, there'd be no Neva a few steps down the hall to keep an eye on Rosie after school. "Rosie," he called.

No answer.

He set the bucket of chicken on the table and headed toward his daughter's room, pausing in the doorway. "Rosie."

"What do you want?" She sat slumped in her desk chair with her back to him, reading a note on her monitor screen.

"It's time for dinner."

"In a minute."

"Now."

The only part of her that moved was her finger on the mouse as she clicked to another screen.

"Rosie."

"What?"

"You didn't set the table."

"I didn't know what time you'd be home."

"I'm home now." He held his breath and grasped for

patience, trying to avoid another fight. Another scene. There'd been far too many of both since her mother had dumped her on his doorstep. "And it's time for dinner. *Now.*"

"Okay." She clicked to a page with a picture of a wild-haired rock guitarist caught in the glare of a gigantic spotlight. A tidal wave of electronic noise flooded the room.

"Turn that off." He stepped through the door. "It'll still be there after you've eaten."

"All right." She blew out a martyred sigh and whirled in her chair to face him. "Chicken again?"

"Yeah."

"Jeez."

"We can go to the store this weekend. You can pick out some things you like to cook."

"I'm not your slave."

"No. You're my daughter," he said, feeling foolish for pointing out the obvious. "And I want you to come and eat your dinner."

"I said all right."

He slid his hands into his pockets and watched her, waiting, praying she'd give in and walk through the door, promising himself he wouldn't move a muscle or say another word until she did. He searched her face— that long, pale face dusted with her mother's freckles and framed with his own dark hair—looking for the sweet, cheerful little girl he'd known so long ago. But she wasn't there.

"Are you just going to stand there all night?" she asked.

"No. Just until you come to dinner."

She rolled her eyes and shoved to her feet. *"Jeez."*

He followed her back to the kitchen, dreading the

nightly routine. Questions about homework, answers he didn't trust. Conversation conducted in monosyllables and resentment hanging so thick in the air it seasoned every bite of food he swallowed. An argument about the cell phone, or bedtime, or something she wanted to buy, or whether a ten-year-old needed a babysitter—anything but the one topic he knew she really wanted to fight over: her mother, and when she was coming back to rescue her.

At times, the pain was unbearable. He wanted to keep his daughter here, with him, wanted to get to know her again, wanted to break through the walls she threw up in his face, wanted his love to matter, to build solid memories for her to take with her when she'd grown and gone. He wanted to gather her close and hold her tight, to make her pain disappear, to feel her thin arms wrap around his neck and hug him tight, the way she'd hugged him so many years ago. A lifetime ago.

But he couldn't take away her hurt, and he couldn't offer the comfort she wanted right now. All he could do was reach deep, deep down below his murky emotions and haul up another handful of patience and love. And pour his invisible offering over the sad and sullen child whose stony expression reminded him of all his failures.

He asked her what she'd done at school that day, but she wasn't talking to him tonight. So they sat in uneasy silence as they picked the meat from the bones.

TESS GLANCED up from her monitor two days later when the door to her office clicked open, admitting a gust of rain-specked wind and a dripping, frowning Quinn. He raked long, scarred fingers through his wet hair and ran an assessing look around her office.

"What are you doing here?" she asked.

"Is that how you greet all your customers?"

"Is that what you are?" she asked as she rose from her chair. "A customer?"

"What kind of customers do you get in here, anyway?" he asked as he stepped farther into the room. His gaze traveled over the sketches pinned to the wall, the fan suspended from the tin ceiling, to the models displayed on tall white cubes and the massive ficus arching over one corner of the red Persian rug on the old plank floor.

"The serious kind." She folded her arms and waited as he leaned over a model of a tasting room she'd designed for a Paso Robles winery.

He straightened and met her stare with a particularly grave expression. "I'm serious."

"Yes," she said as her lips twitched to hide a grin. She wondered if she'd just witnessed a miserly sample of his sense of humor. "You are."

"I like this." He bent again to study the winery model. "It's clean."

"Clean?"

"Uncluttered. French without the frills."

"The client asked for sleek and no-nonsense, with an Old-World feel."

"You gave it to him."

"Giving my clients what they ask for is what keeps me in business."

"Even if you know better than they do what they should be asking for?"

"That's where a touch of diplomacy comes in handy." Tess tilted her head to one side, pleased with his subtle compliments but wondering what he wanted. He had to be working some angle, or he wouldn't have spared the time to stop by. Everyone who knew him said he was a straightforward kind of guy. "It works wonders," she said. "You might give it a try."

"Waste of time." He shoved his hands into his pockets and straightened again, facing her. "I want to change the approach to the parking area. Straight shot, northeast corner."

"The curve from the street on the south will slow traffic and show the building to best advantage. I want visitors to savor their entry into the space." Tess strode to the model set in the wide bay window and pointed to the overlapping layers representing the site grade. "A curving drive will give the landscape design team a more interesting flow to work with. And this bend in the road will be the perfect place for an ornamental tree."

"We can get more parking spaces if we come in straight from the street." He crossed the room to where she stood and sliced a finger across the softly cascading form. "Here."

"We've already provided for the number of parking slots the city required."

"There's room for more."

"No."

He glanced at her. "Now might be a good time to try some of that diplomacy you mentioned."

"I don't have to be diplomatic about this."

"You do if it's not cost-effective."

"Everything I've mentioned is in the budget."

"About that budget." He narrowed his eyes. "There's no room for delays."

"Yes, there is."

"Not enough."

Now it was her turn to aim a dark look in his direction. "Are you planning on inefficiency?"

"No. But weather happens. Shit happens. It always does." He leaned toward her. "If you'd spent any time around a construction site, you'd know that."

"I've spent plenty of time around construction sites," she snapped, temper edging her closer to him, "and I've never had any problems with my budgets."

"Because the contractor covered your butt?"

"Don't worry, Quinn. You're the last person I'd ask to cover any piece of my anatomy."

Too late, she realized the direction the conversation had taken. So, obviously, did Quinn. His gaze dropped to her lips a fraction of an instant before hers dropped to his.

She watched, helplessly fascinated, as one corner of his mouth slowly turned up, deepening the groove in his cheek. Her breath snagged, and she was glad that was only half a smile. She had a feeling the complete version would be devastating.

"Are we going to be doing this every day for the next nine months?" she asked when she could suck in air again.

"Arguing?"

Arguing. That's all he'd been doing. She turned and moved toward her desk to put some distance between them. And tossed her witchiest smile over her shoulder, just to get back at him. "What did you think I meant?"

"We only have to argue when you're wrong," he said, his serious expression back in place, "and too stubborn to admit it."

"I've explained my reasons for keeping the plan the way it is."

"Yeah. Got it. Stubborn."

"It's not stubborn. It's better."

"It's more expensive."

"But worth it. And it's in the budget."

He paused to study her, and she studied him right back, admiring the lean, rugged, oh-so-masculine shape filling out his rumpled jacket and weathered jeans.

"Straightening that drive would trim enough to cover a host of unforeseen delays and cost overruns." He slid his hands back into his pockets. "In addition to providing more parking, which would make the customers happy and earn extra points with the city."

"Very practical."

"And hard to argue with."

"Arguing's rarely all that hard for me." She settled in her chair. "I'm stubborn, remember?"

"Yeah. I remember."

Those sky-blue eyes of his tracked her every move as she crossed her legs and smoothed her short, straight skirt. She swiveled to the left, and she swiveled to the right, giving him an interesting view, waiting for his next salvo.

"All right," he said at last.

"All right?"

"Yeah." He walked to her door. "All right."

"That's it?" She stood so quickly her chair bumped the backs of her knees. "You're leaving?"

"I have a site to clear."

"Oh. Well. All right, then."

He grabbed the knob and then stilled, staring at her. "You sound disappointed."

"I'm not."

"Good. I wouldn't want all my diplomacy to go to waste."

"Is that what you were doing here, Quinn? Being diplomatic?"

"Yeah," he said in his deadpan manner. "Couldn't you tell?"

"Now there's an interesting question." She smiled and shifted her hip over the edge of her desk, enjoying the conversation—and the company—entirely too much. "With any number of equally interesting answers."

"Seems to me all it needed was a yes or no."

She tilted her head. "Or a maybe."

"Like I said. Diplomacy is a waste of time."

"Later, then."

"Yeah." The look he shot her arrowed a blast of heat right through to where it counted. "Later."

GENEVA SETTLED into her favorite booth at the Crescent Inn on Friday after her morning water aerobics class and pulled a smooth linen napkin into her lap.

"The usual, Mrs. Chandler?" asked the waitress.

"Yes, thank you, Missy." Geneva smiled at Gordon Talbot's youngest daughter, amazed she was old enough to be working. Time seemed to pass so quickly these days.

These years.

"Hello, Geneva."

Geneva glanced from her list of the day's specials to see Howard Cobb, real estate developer and member of the city council, frowning at her. "Good afternoon, Howard."

"I wondered if I'd find you here."

"Are you stalking me?" She set her menu aside and gave him her blandest smile. "Should I be disturbed?"

His frown deepened. "Mind if I join you?"

"For lunch?" she asked with just a touch of dismay.

"For a moment. Or two."

"Through the iced-tea course, then," she said as Missy delivered her drink.

He settled heavily into the booth across from her, his oversize belly brushing against the table edge. "You know, there are plenty of folks around here who don't look too kindly on Chandler money forcing things they don't want down their throats."

"What an unpleasant image, considering I was about to order my lunch." She delicately dabbed her napkin to the side of her mouth. "I wonder how many of those same folks are cashing paychecks earned with jobs that Chandler money created for them."

"There's no question your husband and his father did some good things for this community." Howard shifted forward as far as his paunch allowed. "But people who built businesses fifty or sixty years ago didn't have the same kinds of concerns that people do today."

"Are you talking about the businesses, or the building of them?"

"We both know what I'm talking about."

She picked up her tea and sipped. "Then this will be a very short conversation."

"You can't get your way all the time, Geneva."

"You're right, of course, Howard," she said with a thin smile. "I'd be a fool to expect that. And I'm not a fool."

"That's right. That's why you should seriously consider backing off this Tidewaters project while there's still time. It's the right thing to do, and you know it."

"If I thought it was the right thing to do, I would have quit before I started. And certainly before investing so much Chandler money in the development phase."

For months she'd poured funds into the pockets of

marine biologists, geologists and engineers. She'd battled federal agencies, the state's coastal concerns, the city's commissions and committees and codes and several local environmental activist groups. But for too many environmentalists, the objective scientific evidence didn't outweigh their emotions. And for too many politicians, the promise of community benefits didn't compensate for the possible loss of their constituents' support.

Cobb's complexion darkened. "The harm this project will cause to the environment will far outweigh any possible economic benefits."

"That's a strange comment, even for you." Geneva took another sip of her tea. "And particularly strange considering that the environmental impact report and the city's financial analysis indicate precisely the opposite."

"Studies bought and paid for," Howard said as he stabbed a beefy finger at the table. "By you."

"Which doesn't make them wrong. Merely purchased. Another part of the cost benefit noted in that financial analysis."

"Some folks might say that smacks of corruption."

"And some might wonder about the conflict of interest for a city councilman who is involved in the construction of a similar commercial building in a different part of town. A building that may soon be in competition with mine for tenants."

Missy hovered near the table, her order pad in her hand. Howard glared at Geneva as he pushed to the side and exited the booth. "This isn't over."

"Oh, I think it will be, in about nine months," Geneva said pleasantly. "When Tidewaters opens its doors amid a buzz of community curiosity and to the delight of its retail tenants. Tenants who may prefer water-front views and the benefits of tourist foot traffic."

"We'll see about that." He turned and stalked out of the inn, dropping a few bills on his table as he passed it.

"Nasty man," whispered Missy.

"But a good tipper, from the looks of it," Geneva said. "I'm sure he means well."

"Everyone means well when they're trying to get their way."

"Why, Missy," Geneva said as she raised her glass, "may I quote you on that?"

"Only if it's off the record." The waitress shook her head. "I don't want any of that guilty-by-association stuff."

Geneva sipped her tea in silence, feeling wonderfully guilt-free. It seemed there were, after all, a few benefits to having time pass so quickly.

CHAPTER FOUR

QUINN WAS in a foul mood on Monday morning as he headed toward the Tidewaters site. An early-morning conference with Rosie's teacher had left him frazzled and frustrated and a bit shaky. Mrs. Thao had told him his daughter wasn't working up to her potential. When he'd examined samples of Rosie's classwork, he'd discovered she wasn't working much at all. Half-finished math papers, half-assed compositions.

Turning down Front Street, he muttered a curse. He could check her homework for completion; he couldn't monitor what she did in the classroom. And he couldn't expect Mrs. Thao to fuss over Rosie, one-on-one. Rosie would have to quit her game of slow-motion sabotage or risk failing the year. He'd have to lay down the law, arrange to check in with her teacher on a regular basis, show his daughter he could be damn stubborn when it came to succeeding at something that mattered.

Just what they both needed: more tension at home.

He'd hoped Rosie would have begun to settle down, to resign herself to the situation and the fact she'd be staying with him for a while. Quite a while, if he could make it stick. But it seemed she'd decided to shut down in addition to shutting him out. And he didn't know how to reach her.

Maybe he needed some help. Maybe that was what they both needed.

Too bad the idea tangled his gut and yanked on the knots. His morning coffee nearly bored a hole in his stomach lining at the thought of seeing a counselor. Rosie might shift tactics to open rebellion. Nancy would probably use it as a weapon in a custody battle. And he damn well didn't want to dredge up all the bitter mistakes of his own past, just when he was able to focus on the future.

He swung into the job site, ready to sweep aside the mess of his personal life and concentrate on work he knew how to do, with tools he knew how to wield. Ready to make tangible progress to offset his failures.

He expected to see Rusty, one of his crew members, digging footings with Quinn Construction's brand-new backhoe while Trap and Wylie Lundgren cleared the rest of the site with their excavating equipment. Instead, he saw the Lundgrens standing with his own men near the backhoe. Rusty trudged toward Quinn's truck, a frown on his face and worry in his eyes.

With another muttered curse, Quinn grabbed his tool belt and hard hat, stepped out and slammed the truck door. "Problem?"

Rusty's cheek bulged as he shifted his habitual wad of gum. "Yep. With the backhoe."

"What kind of problem?"

"Best have a look for yourself."

Quinn followed him toward the equipment, nodding at the wiry, grizzled Lundgren brothers as he passed. "Morning, Trap. Wylie."

Trap answered with a scowl. "Too bad it's such a pisser."

Quinn strapped on his belt and stared at the men loitering around the equipment, wasting valuable time. "What's going on here?"

"Take a look," Rusty said again.

Quinn leaned in to peer at the engine. Grains of sand lay scattered over the engine block. "What the hell?"

"It seized up a few seconds after I switched on the ignition. Figure the bastard poured sand in the oil filter." Easygoing Rusty had murder in his eyes. "He didn't have to look too far. We're standing in a yard full of the stuff."

Sand in the oil filter meant sand spreading through the engine—scoring the pistons, ruining the chambers and turning the entire engine into a worthless hunk of metal.

An expensive hunk of metal. Quinn began running the figures in his head, estimating the costs of delays on the site, the time lost on paperwork and the added expense of a rental to replace this piece. The long-range damage to his insurance rates. Fury surged through him as he slowly straightened and scanned the rest of the equipment on the site. "Anything else wrecked?"

"Nope." Wylie lifted the rim of his gimme cap to scratch at his forehead with grimy fingers. "Everything else seems okay. And we aim to keep it that way."

"What does that mean?"

"Means we're going to be trailering our equipment off-site every evening. We can't afford to lose one of our machines to some crazy dude who thinks dumping sand in an engine is an evening's entertainment."

Trailering fees hadn't been included in the Lundgrens' subcontracting bid for the excavations. Quinn figured they'd tack on the added expense when they sent the bill. He nodded, his gut on fire as he took another hit. "All right, then."

He glanced at the operators. "Let's get going here. Rusty, Jim, get a cable hooked to the backhoe and haul it up on that trailer. I want the rest of the building site cleared for the footings by the end of the day."

He waited while Trap and Wylie moved off to their excavator and bulldozer and the rest of the men got back to work. And then he trudged over to his office trailer, jogged up the steps and shut the door behind him. He pulled his cell phone from a pocket and paused, pinching the bridge of his nose. A headache was coming on, riding a wave of anxiety.

And then the dark, seductive need flowed in beneath it, urging him to walk out of his office, climb into his pickup, drive away from his troubles and find a few moments of peace. His crew could take it from here. Wylie and Trap—they knew what to do. Hell, what if he'd phoned in sick? The work would still get done. Time to himself, that's all he needed. No one would know or care if he took a drink to settle his nerves. Just one. One hour, one drink.

A bead of sweat trickled down his spine as he battled away the demons buzzing inside. Steady, steady. Breathe. Think.

Damn, damn, damn.

He stared at the phone lying like a lump of lead in his palm, struggling for the strength to make a call. The crisis passed, and he slumped against the counter, feeling bruised and sour and old as dust. He willed himself to concentrate on the job, to plan for some action that would drag him back into the real world, the world outside his shaky, hollow being.

Wylie's bulldozer rumbled past the office, vibrating the thin metal walls and sloshing the cold coffee in the mug beside Quinn's elbow. The familiar odors of diesel exhaust and fresh-turned clay floated through the air, and the productive clang and roar of the excavator hung in the background. He needed to call the police—yes, call and file a report about what had happened here this morning. But before he made that call, there was someone else who had to be notified. Someone who could help clear his mind and get him on track again, to do what he needed to do today.

He took another deep breath and punched in a number from memory. "Geneva," he said when she picked up. "It's Quinn. Sorry to be calling so early."

AFTER MEETING Addie at her shop to discuss wedding-shower plans over takeout salads, Tess hadn't planned on extending her lunch break in Dee Ketchum's Pink Boutique. But she'd paused to drool over the cutest pair of shell-studded flip-flops arranged in Dee's shop window. And after she'd spied a vintage-style purse with shimmering beads fanning in the colors of a peacock's tail, she hadn't been able to resist stepping in to peek at the price tag. And once she'd walked into the tiny store, she'd decided she might as well take a few minutes to check out the other tempting items Dee might have tucked inside her treasure-box store.

And wasn't it a good thing she'd taken the time to drape that gauzy, cherry-dotted scarf over the black boat-neck sweater she was carrying to the dressing room? She might not have overheard Celia Kulstad telling Dee about the patrol car she'd seen parked at the Tidewaters site that morning.

Now Tess was speeding toward the waterfront, her cell phone to her ear, waiting for Geneva to pick up. She braked and skidded to a stop, clicking her nails on the steering wheel as Crazy Ed lumbered across the street, headed to the marina. He waved and gave her a gap-toothed grin, and she waggled her fingers in response. "Get a move on, Eddie boy," she said. "I'm in a hurry here."

When she got Geneva's voice mail, she tossed the phone into her purse, her irritation growing. She'd rather talk with Grandmère about this in person, anyway. Later, when her temper had eased a bit. Or when it had ratcheted higher, if she discovered Quinn had handed her a reason to give him some grief.

A few moments later she jerked to a stop at the edge of the site and stepped from her car. Trap Hunter's excavating equipment chugged and roared and clawed at the ground, tearing through the reddish-brown earth with steel talons. Beyond the ragged ditches of the footings, one of Quinn's crew—Ned Landreau, she thought—nudged an elbow into Quinn's ribs as he leaned to gaze through a laser level.

Quinn straightened and waited, his pose casual and his expression grim as Tess picked her way across yards of tracked-up, clodding earth. Her heels sank into the pungent soil, coating her navy slingbacks with grime, and she cursed him with every shoe-sucking step.

Especially since the way Quinn looked, with his muscular form outlined by the fabric of his chambray shirt and his tool belt slung low over one jean-clad hip, nearly made her mouth go dry.

"Glad you could make it," he said after she'd detoured around the deep gash of the western footing. "But you might want to rethink your choice of outfits if you're going to make a habit of dropping by. Things can get pretty messy around a construction site."

She swiped a speck of mud from her pencil-slim skirt and tugged at her coordinating shantung-silk jacket. "I wasn't planning on stopping by. I heard the police were here this morning. And I've been around plenty of construction sites."

"Good. Then I won't have to remind you to bring a hard hat. I don't have one to spare." He turned back to his level, squinted into the scope and gestured to a crew member holding a marker near a footing.

She took another careful step closer. "Why was a patrol car here?"

"Because I called to file a report."

"About what?"

"Vandalism."

"What?"

He paused and leisurely added a note to his clipboard, but the ripple of muscle along the edge of his jaw betrayed the effort he was making to control his anger. "Someone poured some sand in an oil filter."

"That sounds serious."

He flicked a frigid glance in her direction. "It is."

"What do you intend to do about it?"

"Rent another backhoe until I can get mine fixed."

"I mean," she said as she folded her arms across her chest, "what are you going to do about getting better security so this kind of thing won't happen again?"

"What do you mean, security?" He shifted closer and angled his head toward hers. "Are you suggesting I hire a guard?"

She held her ground, though she could nearly feel the temper and heat pumping off him. "Pouring sand in an engine is a lot more serious than the typical mischief at a site like this. Things like graffiti or materials theft."

"I know what goes on at sites like this."

"It could happen again."

"I know that, too."

"Tell me," she said sweetly, "is there anything you don't know?"

The corners of his mouth turned up in an unfriendly grin, and his gaze roamed over her features. "Plenty. Particularly about female architects."

"If I were you," she said, recklessly following the shift in the argument, "I'd be in a big hurry to figure things out."

His eyes darkened. "What makes you think I'm not?"

He bent again at the waist and squinted into the scope. Tess was proud of herself for not noticing the way the back of his jeans curved behind his tool belt.

"Look, Quinn, I—"

"If you don't think I can handle this job, well, you're entitled to your opinion." He made an adjustment to the level and checked the scope again. "But you're not the one who hired me to do it. And the woman who did hire me wants us to work together."

"Believe me, I'm aware of that."

"So work with me."

He shot one of his penetrating looks at her, the one that made her feel as though he could see deep inside her to that place where she hid all her doubts and insecurities. She detested that look, nearly as much as she detested the fact that he was right. She had to work with him.

"Fine," she said. "I'll work with you. And I'll expect the same. A phone call when there's something—*any-thing*—to report."

He nodded solemnly. "You got it."

"Now, about the security—"

"Already taken care of." He called another instruction to the man with the marker. "I discussed it with Geneva."

His words stung like a slap. Tess tried not to show it, to keep her eyes on his, but she knew from the way his frown deepened that he'd noted her flinch.

"Well," she said when she'd recovered, "now you can discuss it with me."

"Look, Tess, this isn't—"

"Later. At my office. Five o'clock." She turned on her soggy, muddy heel and walked away.

STILL in a temper a quarter of an hour later, Tess shoved her way into her office and then swore when her Macho-Mex mocha sloshed over the edge of the cup. Chocolate spatters layered over the dusty red splotches on her slingbacks. "Aww, for cryin' out—"

The phone on her desk rang, and she carefully speed-walked to the back of the room, holding the coffee at arm's length. "Roussel Designs, Tess Roussel speaking."

"You've obviously made it back to work," Geneva said with a hint of sarcasm.

"Not all my work is done in the office." Tess set the cup on the desk and reached for a tissue to wipe her hand. "Thank you for returning my call."

"Anytime, dear."

Tess frowned as she toed off her shoes. Her grandmother didn't sound all that upset by what had happened at Tidewaters that morning. Not that she wanted her grandmother to be upset—not unless she was upset with Quinn. Then she could erupt like a Fourth of July fireworks display and fire his nicely shaped ass. "I wanted to touch base with you about what happened at the site this morning."

"The vandalism," Geneva said with a disgusted sigh.

"Yes." Tess tucked the phone between her ear and shoulder and snatched another tissue from her apple-red dispenser. "I understand Quinn has already discussed everything with you."

"Yes, he has. It's all terribly distressing, all the trouble and expense involved in setting things right. But he assures me there won't be any delays. And he's handled everything quite satisfactorily, with no need for your attention."

"He may not have needed it, but he got it." Tess picked up one of her shoes and began to scrub at the stains. "Finding out from one of the shopkeepers downtown that the police had been called to Tidewaters got my attention pretty damn quick."

"Really, Tess, must you use that kind of language?"

"I beg your pardon. Sorry." She chipped a nail on her shoe heel and swore under her breath as she tossed the soiled, crumpled tissue toward her waste bin. The wad bounced off the rim and tumbled to the floor. This just wasn't her day. "I tend to get upset when my job site is the scene of a criminal investigation, and I'm not notified."

"Although I appreciate your enthusiasm for this project," Geneva said in a terrifyingly frigid tone, "I must remind you that Tidewaters belongs to me, not to you."

Tess stiffened and dropped the shoe. "Yes, Mémère."

"You may be my granddaughter, but you are also, where Tidewaters is concerned, my employee."

It was that fact, more than her grandmother's scolding, that heated Tess's cheeks with embarrassment and guilt. An angry phone call wasn't the best way to display her professional abilities to her biggest client to date.

She detested being caught making an error in judgment. She despised weakness, especially in herself, and she loathed the shriveling remorse that swamped her at times like this. That was why she worked so hard, took such care, fussed over the details. Stayed in control. There were fewer mistakes that way.

She shut her eyes and rubbed her forehead. "I want— I *need*—to be kept in the loop. I have to be a part of this, each step of it, all the way through. It's not just the way I want it. It's my job. And if I'm going to do a good job, I need to be informed about everything—all the progress and all the problems."

"I don't suppose," Geneva said, "it would do any good to ask you to be civil to Quinn when you discuss this with him."

"I can be civil." Tess slowly sank into her chair. "I can be anything I want to be."

"Except punctual."

"Except that." Her smile was faint. "But I'm working on it."

"Good. Now," Geneva said with a brisk change of tone, "I have some unrelated news I think will please you."

"About Charlie's wedding shower?" Tess had left an earlier phone message asking if she could host the party at Chandler House. Tess's own house was too small for the event she had in mind, and Addie's apartment was literally a hole in the wall behind her shop.

"About her wedding," Geneva said.

"Her wedding?"

"I've offered Maudie the opportunity to hold Charlie's wedding here. There's plenty of space in the garden, near the pergola."

"I'm sure she was thrilled. Charlie will be, too." Tess swiveled in her chair and stared out her windows, seeing white chairs in neat lines and pastel ribbons twined with wisteria instead of the pale wisps of late-afternoon fog drifting across Main Street. "And that means the pressure's on now. Charlie will have to choose a summer date."

"That's what Maudie and I thought, too."

"She didn't have a chance, not with you two plotting against her." Tess grinned. "Besides, who wouldn't want a wedding at Chandler House?"

"My granddaughter, for one."

Tess released a silent sigh. They'd had this discussion before. "I never said I didn't want to get married there."

"You never said you wanted to get married."

"There are things I need to do before I'm ready to think about it. And one of those things is finding a man I want to marry."

"Find one," Geneva ordered as if she were instructing her gardener where to place a rosebush. "Before I get too old to dance at the reception."

Tess grinned. "Yes, Mémère."

CHAPTER FIVE

QUINN GUIDED his pickup to the curb outside Tess's office door a few minutes before five o'clock and switched off the ignition. He sat in the cab for a moment, banking his temper. It had been a long, frustrating day, and there was plenty of it left—he still had to fix dinner, start a load of laundry and deal with Rosie. But first he had to go another round with the only woman he knew who could scramble his thoughts and senses until he forgot how much he wanted a drink.

She'd been wearing a dark blue suit today, and something that made her smell like a bucket stuffed with flowers. Fresh, white flowers drooping with early-morning water drops, like those tiny, bell-shaped flowers sprouting up from a mass of fat, grassy green in the shade under Mrs. Brubaker's maple tree.

And pearls, for God's sake. On the site. Dangling from her pretty pink ears and slipping and sliding between her breasts. With the rumble and clang of Trap's excavator and the diesel stench of Wylie's bulldozer failing to block the punches she'd landed on his senses.

She sure knew how to push his buttons—coming to the job in that getup, distracting his crew, arguing with him in public, questioning his judgment. And crawling under his skin, making him so hard he'd had to keep bending over and peering through the level's scope as if his life depended on what he could see across the footings.

Once she'd left and he'd cooled off, he'd had to acknowledge her point. But the fact was, he'd owed Geneva a phone call. She was the client. The owner. He'd need to meet with her later, to discuss the details and negotiate the financing for the site's security.

Still, he supposed he should have called Tess.

Which only pissed him off again.

With a curse, he exited his truck. Rue Matson waved as she locked up her tiny gardening shop, and he nodded as he stepped up onto the curb. How someone could make a living selling birdseed and fancy shovels was a mystery. "Evening, Rue."

"It's a pretty one, isn't it?" She squinted at a faded blue sky dotted with dingy white clouds and then glanced at the flower boxes tucked below Tess's three-sided office window. "Nearly as pretty as those arrangements. Tess sure knows how to put a planter together. There's a trick to doing it right, you know."

"Is there?"

"Oh, yes." Rue rambled on in her friendly shop-keeper voice about color and texture and layers and a bunch of other things Quinn didn't care about. But he had to admit, as he waved goodbye to Rue, that they were pretty planters. As sassy and colorful as the woman who'd planted them.

And he had to admit, as he stalked through her door, that Tess had made her office space pretty, too. Not too fussy, not too plain. Not too much emphasis on the business, but enough drawings and models to give a quick impression of competence and skill. Just right, just the way an architect's office should look. The woman had class.

She was also sitting too close to Don Gladdings, who had pulled a visitor's chair to Tess's side of the desk. Don was taking advantage of his maneuver to lean over her shoulder and peer at something on her computer monitor, while she made her pitch for redrawing a section of his new car dealership. Clever phrases delivered with a subtle appeal to Don's pride in his business—architectural design as ego gratification.

Quinn wondered whether Don was enjoying that white-flower smell, too. He cleared his throat in an overly loud cough.

Tess raised her eyes to Quinn's, and his temper shifted into a lower gear, somewhere near basic agitation. Hard to stay ticked off at a woman who could aim a scorched-dagger glance while wearing ice-cool pearls.

"I'll be with you in a few minutes," she said.

Quinn grunted a response and tucked his hands into his pockets as he started a slow turn of the outer office area. It was a waste of energy staying angry about small, stupid things. There were far more important items needing far more of his energy at the moment. Rosie. Security at the job site. Scheduling around the equipment hassles.

If Tess wanted to drag him down to her turf, to stage a showdown on her own territory, he could shrug it off. After all, it was a smart move. He'd have done the same, in her place.

He sneaked a glance at her and watched her direct Don's attention to some detail on her monitor with polish-slicked nails on the ends of long, ringless fingers. The lady had spunk.

And talent to spare. Quinn paused to study her model of Tidewaters, once again admiring the blend of sleek lines and traditional charm, the clever use of space and the integration with the setting. Why she chose to squander her gifts on projects here in Carnelian Cove, he wasn't quite sure.

But he sure was glad she'd decided to stick around for a while.

The realization rattled him. He waited for his feelings to sort themselves out and settle down inside, worried that this latest complicated thought might mess up the points he intended to make about this morning's argument. Well, he'd find a way to shrug off this sneaky soft spot, too. When it came to Tess Roussel, he'd be wise keeping his edge.

Besides, he didn't know all that much about her. He'd heard she came from money on both sides, but from what he'd observed, she didn't seem to have much of her own. There were nicer offices available in the Cove. And he knew—because curiosity had driven him past it one night—that she'd settled for one of the basic tract houses lining the streets in the newer section east of town. Her car was anything but basic, but it was an older model.

Maybe she needed this job as much as he did. Maybe that explained the flicker of desperation he thought he'd detected behind that bewitching stare of hers.

Don stood and dragged his chair back into place, and Tess walked him to her door. "Gotta watch out for this lady," Don said as he passed Quinn. "She'll have you wanting things you never knew you needed until she mentions them."

"But you do need them. And isn't it nice to have someone fuss over all those details for you?" Tess gave Don a dazzling smile, and his face lit up in obvious agreement.

Poor sucker.

She waved goodbye to her customer, closed and locked her door, flipped the Open sign to Closed and turned to face Quinn. "Thanks for coming," she said in her crisp, uptown voice. "Can I get you something to drink? Coffee?"

"No. Thanks."

She gave the bottom of her shiny blue jacket a sharp tug in the habit he recognized as her down-to-business attitude adjustment. Moving to the scrawny counter suspended on the wall behind her desk, she poured something into a pretty cup painted with little purple flowers.

"Only kids drink stuff like that," he said as she added a ridiculous amount of sugar.

"I have a sweet tooth." She settled her hip against the desk's edge and raised the cup to her lips. "And a metabolism that lets me indulge it."

He watched her full red lips pucker around the cup rim, and his own system kicked up a notch. "You'd better make this fast," he warned, "'cause I've got plans for this evening."

"Plans involving the security at the site?"

"That's right."

"What are you going to do, exactly?"

He pulled his hands from his pockets so he could curl his fingers into fists. "You didn't ask your grandmother?"

"I'm asking you." She blushed and lowered the cup to its saucer, and the china rattled as she set down the pieces. "Geneva Chandler may be my grandmother, but on this job she's my boss."

"That's a cozy arrangement."

"In case you haven't noticed, she doesn't play favorites."

"No, she doesn't," he said. "When it comes to business, she's too smart to play any kind of game."

Her breath snagged with a tiny flinch, and he caught a glimpse of a shadowy flicker in her eyes—a brief softening that hinted at a vulnerability that intrigued him. And in the next moment, before he could guess at its cause, it was gone.

He'd figured she didn't have too many chinks in her armor. And now that he'd found one, he was sure to regret it. He preferred the straightforward Tess, the model-in-the-window version who could be relied on to keep her chin up and her talk on target.

While he considered the flaws in his theory, he discovered they'd somehow shifted closer to each other during their conversation. Too close. He needed to take a step back, but he didn't want to give any ground.

He narrowed his eyes, daring her to make the first move, to retreat or…something else. But then her lips curled up at the edges, and he knew she wouldn't give him the satisfaction. She crossed her arms beneath her breasts, one wrist brushing against him as she built her little barrier, staying within firing range while giving him a shot of her perfume.

Potent stuff. He crammed his hands back into his pockets so he wouldn't put them somewhere they didn't belong.

"There are two businesswomen in this deal," she said. "You might have an easier time on this job if you remembered that fact."

"Believe me, that fact is a tough one to forget."

He inched back, giving them both some space. What he was about to say required some distance. "And so is the fact that I want you."

"I know." Her catlike smile reappeared. "I'd prefer it if you respected me, or cared—just a bit—about me. But I can work with a simple case of lust."

"Good to know." *Damn.* He sure did like her direct approach and her feisty attitude. And he supposed he liked Tess a bit, too. He hadn't been ready to confess to that particular fact, but there it was, right up front. Just like her.

A guy had to appreciate a woman who could lay it out straight and level.

"Good to know that fact won't be keeping you up nights," he said.

"Oh, but I'm hoping it'll come to that." She tilted her head to one side, toying with him. "Aren't you?"

"Is that an invitation?"

"Do you have to ask?"

"No." He smiled, enjoying this particular game.

She glanced over his shoulder and frowned. "Oh, hell," she said as she dashed toward her door. "I'll be right back."

He walked to the front of her office to watch the scene outside the bay window. Tess paced a tight circuit on the sidewalk, her temper on display as she gestured from her car to the meter near one headlight. It was obvious her arguments were failing to score any points with the uniformed woman calmly filling out a form on her notepad. Tess took the piece of paper, gave the woman a parting scowl and stomped back inside.

"Parking ticket?" Quinn asked as the slammed door set the tiny bell overhead dancing and ringing.

"Clever deduction." Tess wadded the paper and stuffed it in a pocket.

"Why don't you park in one of the alley spaces?"

"I don't have one."

"One should come with the lease." He frowned. "Talk to your landlord."

"I did. He needed the space for another tenant, and I traded for a reduction in my rent."

"Seems to me you're spending your discount on fines."

"I don't need you to point that out." She batted her hair out of her eyes with a disgusted sigh. "Besides, it's the principle of the thing. There shouldn't be any parking meters in the marina district."

"I thought the meters raised revenue for the city."

"But this is a tourist area. We should be encouraging tourism—and trade—in the city's most historic area."

"Doesn't seem to me the meters are as much of a hindrance to the tourists," he said, "as are the merchants who take all the available curbside parking."

The look she gave him nearly blasted a layer off his hide. "As I said," she reminded him, "it's the principle of the thing. And I didn't bother setting my alarms because I didn't think I'd still be here this late."

With an effort, he suppressed a smile. "Alarms?"

"Don't ask," she said with another hide-threatening look.

"All right." He shrugged. "You're the one who called this meeting, not me."

"Thank you so much for pointing that out."

His smile faded. "I'm thinking of fencing in the site."

Her expression went blank for a second, and then she straightened and gave her jacket another tiny tug. "How much is that going to cost?"

"More than what was budgeted."

"There's nothing budgeted for a fence."

"There you go," he said.

"How will you pay for it?"

"The only way I know how."

"Geneva."

He didn't answer, and he could practically see her squirm. She didn't want to go begging to her grandmother any more than he did. But one of them would have to do it.

"It probably won't prevent any more vandalism," he said. "Anyone serious about getting in and causing trouble will still be able to do it. But it would make it a hell of a lot easier to collect on an insurance claim if anything else happens."

"Right." She sighed and nodded. "Okay. Make sure I get a key."

He nodded and turned toward the door.

"And don't forget to keep me updated on everything. *Everything*," she added as she scooted past him to grab the knob. "Quinn."

He stopped and stared at her, allowing himself to imagine lapping her up as if she were a sugary drink. No harm in looking. No harm in talking, in playing the kind of game where two adults laid their cards on the table. They both knew the score. "Yeah," he said. "I know you want me, too."

"Good to hear," she said as she turned the knob. "I like to keep things neat and tidy."

He inhaled deeply as he passed her, breathing in her white-flower scent as he stepped into the street. And then he climbed into his truck and made a fast U-turn and a faster getaway.

CHAPTER SIX

FRIDAY AFTERNOON, nearly two weeks after the vandalism incident at the job site, Tess taped a gone-for-the-day note to one of her front windows. Any other time, she'd have given her new pair of Matisse sandals—the ones with the darling polka-dot bows and the sexy ankle straps—to have a client drop in with a request for her immediate assistance with a design. But today she didn't want to be trapped in her office whipping up a set of revised elevations for a discount furniture warehouse. Today Tidewaters' foundation was being poured, and she wanted to be there to witness every moment.

Feeling like a mother whose toddler was about to take its first steps, she checked her quilted print tote to make sure she'd packed her camera. And then she flipped her Open sign over to Closed and locked her office door before heading down Main Street toward the small public lot where she'd parked her car.

Things were definitely looking up. Besides sketching the last-minute elevations, she'd consulted with another potential client about a family house and met with a contractor at a commercial site across town. She couldn't be one hundred percent certain that the big white sign Quinn had erected at Tidewaters—the one featuring Tess Roussel, Architect in neat block lettering—was driving new business her way, but with that possibility and the recent break in the weather, she was suddenly busier than she'd hoped she might be. Perhaps next month, if her customers paid their bills on time, she could avoid dipping into her savings to pay her own.

She swung her tote onto the passenger seat, slid into her car and sped down Main Street, eager to get back to the waterfront and check out the finish work on the concrete slabs. Charlie had called a quarter of an hour ago to report that the final Keene mixer truck had delivered its load. Tess knew she wouldn't be seeing anything she hadn't already seen on other sites many times before, but she'd already missed more of the day's events than she'd intended. She'd been at the site before seven that morning, watching while Quinn's crew put the final touches on the foundation forms and waiting for the first mixer to appear. And she'd stopped by at lunchtime with a big pink box of Marie-Claudette's brownies and six-packs of soft drinks.

Now she figured it was time for a coffee break, so she pulled through one of her favorite drive-throughs to buy enough for everyone at the site. And since coffee alone was never enough in the middle of the afternoon, she stopped in at Bern's Bakery again to purchase a dozen apple fritters. The snacks weren't bribes for Quinn's crew; they were a legitimate part of today's celebration.

Lately she'd made a habit of driving past the site early each morning on her way to work, and late every afternoon at the end of her business day. The groundwork was progressing well and in an orderly fashion— Quinn maintained a clean site.

But not once had she found an opportunity to have the place to herself. It seemed Quinn was always there.

He stayed late, working with a skeleton crew after regular hours. And he showed up early on Saturday and kept at it on into the weekend. She'd even spied his pickup parked near the foundation forms on Sunday afternoon when she'd detoured to the waterfront on a drive-through mocha run. As far as she could see, the man had no life outside the job.

She had to admit she was impressed by the way he worked beside his men—no drive-by supervision or watching from the sidelines for Quinn. Which meant he must squeeze in the paperwork late at night or before dawn.

She could have stopped and asked how things were going, in a friendly manner, instead of scooting past. It would probably improve their business relationship if she'd make an appearance and mention her admiration for what Quinn had accomplished in near-record time. Still, she'd prefer to check on the site when he wasn't there.

It wasn't because she was uncomfortable with what they'd discussed in her office that Monday afternoon following the vandalism incident. There was no point in ignoring the mutual attraction, especially if there was a chance they could enjoy the possible benefits without gumming up the work. A pretty slim chance, given the fact that he hadn't made a move in her direction, even after she'd given him the green light.

No, it was because the man made her uncomfortable with his impassive stare and his unnatural stillness. And she didn't want to hand him an excuse to accuse her of sticking her nose in where it didn't belong.

Even if her nose had a right to be stuck in any place she chose to stick it at Tidewaters.

Several blocks from the bakery, Tess parked her

roadster between a row of pickups and the pump operator's boom truck. Before collecting the coffee and pastries, she brushed back her bangs and then pulled on the second layer of a matched-sweater set that coordinated with the casual tan slacks she'd chosen for today's wardrobe challenges. And then she carefully picked her way across the muddy job site in her pretty new low-heeled boots, careful to avoid the worst of the mud.

Circling around a stack of rebar, she paused near the ridiculously handsome driver washing out a Keene Concrete mixer. "Shorthanded today?"

"Nope." Jack Maguire flashed a deeply dimpled grin at her as he sprayed the chute. "Spying."

"Didn't Charlie give you a full report?" Her friend had delivered the first load early this morning.

"Can't let her have all the fun. I wanted to check on things for myself." He stepped to the side and hung the hose on its hook. "And I wanted to personally deliver a dinner invitation. For tonight, if you can manage to pry yourself away from all the excitement here. I know it'll be tough. There's nothing like watching concrete setting up…unless it's watching grass growing."

"That depends on the concrete. This happens to be mine. In a supervisory sense, anyway."

"You're not going to mark your initials in it, are you?"

"*Please.* I'm a professional. I've got a stamp. Just kidding," she added when Jack shot her a quizzical look.

"I figured. I didn't think Quinn would let you pull a stunt like that, anyway."

She ignored the reference to the contractor and lifted the bag of fritters. "Are you cooking?"

Jack nodded as he pulled off his gloves to take one of the pastries Tess offered. "Extra-thick steaks, my country-bean salad and a bottle of Napa Valley champagne. To celebrate Tidewaters' foundation."

Tess turned to study the view, her heart swelling with pride and anticipation. Wide, slick surfaces of gray concrete spread along the bay's shore, boxed in by stake-studded forms. Quinn's crew guided the power trowels, smoothing the surface as it hardened.

"Sounds good," she said. "But I want to stay here until they're finished."

"I reckoned that might be the case. Looks to me like they've just about wrapped things up." Jack stuffed the last bite of fritter into his mouth before removing the chutes and placing them on their hangers. "Another hour or two, then, at most. No problem. We'll wait till you and Quinn show up."

"Quinn?"

"He's invited, too. Come on, Tess," Jack said when he noticed her scowl. "He's a big part of this, too."

"And one of your biggest customers." She felt a pout coming on, damn it. She'd promised herself she wouldn't waste any emotional energy on Quinn this week, but she wasn't having much success with the resentment part of the bargain.

"That's right," Jack said. "Wouldn't hurt to let him know just how much Keene Concrete appreciates his business."

She glanced toward the office trailer where Quinn stood with a clipboard, paging through a thick stack of papers. "I guess I could tolerate his company for one evening."

"Big of you," Jack said. "And safe. Charlie says he'll probably turn me down. He's got a daughter waiting for him at home."

"He does?"

She didn't understand why the thought of Quinn as a parent should knock her off balance. She'd heard a few vague references to his divorce—bitter, was her impression—and more than one person had mentioned something about a kid. People in Carnelian Cove discussed each other's business; they always had. But few of them, it seemed, had much to say about Quinn—maybe because he had so little to say about himself. Or anything at all, for that matter.

Still, she'd assumed his daughter was living with her mother.

Jack tossed his gloves in the truck's cab. "Must be tough running a business and taking care of a kid all on his own."

"Women do it all the time."

"Tough for them, too."

He leaned a shoulder against his truck in one of his casual poses. "You don't like him much, do you?"

"Quinn?" Tess shifted the bags in her arms. "Define *much*."

"At all."

She shrugged. "Personality conflict. No, wait—that can't be it. He'd have to have a personality for that to cause a problem."

Jack shook his head. "I sure do feel sorry for the guy."

"Because he has to work with me?"

Jack avoided answering her question by flicking a fingertip affectionately down the tip of her nose. "Maybe we'll discover he has a personality at dinner tonight."

"If he agrees to come."

"Leave it to me," Jack said as he climbed into the cab, drenching his words in his thickest South Carolina accent. "I'll talk him into it."

The mixer's engine roared to life, and Tess stepped back as Jack pulled away. If anyone could persuade Quinn to be sociable for an evening, it was syrup-tongued Jack Maguire.

She turned and continued toward the foundation forms, pausing near a plank-and-sawhorse table to hand steaming cups of coffee to Phil and Ned. As she chatted with the men and set down the bakery bag beside the cardboard coffee carrier, she noticed Quinn look her way, fixing that laserlike gaze on her as if he were locking on target.

What would it be like to be the object of that startlingly acute focus in bed?

She rubbed her hands over her arms and wandered toward the southwestern corner of the foundation, where his crew had begun the pour that morning. With every step, she was aware of those piercing blue eyes tracking her movements, making her skin tingle with a prickly sensation that had nothing to do with the chilling breeze blowing in off the bay. Would Quinn manage to be pleasant tonight, if he came to Charlie's house for dinner? Or would he stare at her across the table, upsetting her stomach and torturing her with a different kind of hunger?

She wasn't sure she wanted to discover whether he could be relaxed and charming. She was having plenty of trouble dealing with him here, in a work setting, where she was supposed to be in control. As much in control of the situation as she could manage, considering she'd spent most of her time trying to avoid him.

This was not how she normally conducted her affairs, business or otherwise. This was no way to get a building constructed the way she wanted it, and it was no way to maintain the upper hand in a personal relationship—if they were going to have one.

She turned to face Quinn, meeting and holding his stare, before he frowned and lowered his gaze to the paperwork in his hands. Score one for Roussel.

It was a silly game, and suddenly she was tired of playing it. Tired of keeping score. It was time to take charge of the situation. She could begin by being relentlessly reasonable and charming this evening, whether Quinn liked it or not.

TESS SAT at Charlie's kitchen table at seven-thirty that evening, slicing bread for bruschetta. Her friend stood at the sink, cleaning potatoes to bake in the microwave. "Did you hear that?" asked Tess. "Did you?"

"If you're going to complain again about your stomach growling," Charlie said, "I'm going to cram this potato in your whiny mouth."

"Never mind, then. Just ignore the starving guest in the corner. The one who's helping prepare the meal." Tess heaved a theatrical sigh and sawed through another length of sourdough. "What time is it, anyway?"

"Two minutes since the last time you asked." Charlie wiped her hands with a dish towel and crossed the room to gaze through the window. No doubt she was checking on Jack, who'd been sent to scrub the grill under Hardy's supervision. "Quinn can't help it if he's running late. He had to arrange for dinner and a sitter for his daughter, and he said he wanted to swing by the site to check on things again on his way here."

His daughter. Tess struggled for a moment, caught between stubborn pride and curiosity. Only for a moment. "How old is she?"

"Quinn's daughter?"

"No. The sitter." Tess rolled her eyes. "Is she in elementary school? Junior high?"

"Elementary. Nine? Ten, maybe?" Charlie returned to the sink and picked up another potato. "You know, you could always ask him when he gets here."

"It doesn't matter. What?" Tess asked when Charlie's mouth twitched up at one corner. "What are you thinking?"

"That you have this strange and complicated thing for Quinn."

"That's absurd. The man's a walking minefield."

"I know. That's why you're attracted to him."

Tess sighed again and reached for the mozzarella. "I hate to be so predictable."

"It's better than being complicated." Charlie dumped the potatoes on a baking dish. "Or touching off an explosion that might maim a couple of innocent bystanders."

Tess set aside the knife. "You don't approve."

Charlie's lips pressed in a thin, straight line. "I like you both. I don't want to see either of you get hurt."

"Why would I get hurt?" Tess began to arrange the sliced bread on a cookie sheet. "I'm the one in charge in this situation, and Quinn knows it."

"I'm not talking about the work."

"You can't seriously be talking about anything else." She drizzled olive oil over the slices. "Because there isn't anything else worth discussing. And there won't be."

"All right. Fine."

"I don't go looking for complicated, you know." Tess stole a sliver of cheese while Charlie wasn't looking and popped it into her mouth. "I prefer to love 'em and leave 'em on friendly terms. It's so easy with the easy men, the guys who are looking for an uncomplicated time with an uncomplicated woman. I just get bored sometimes with the same old, same old. I like a challenge every once in a while."

Charlie's frown deepened. "Which makes me think you're suddenly interested in a certain difficult single father."

"Which makes me wonder why you invited us both to dinner tonight."

"Jack's idea." Charlie leaned an elbow on the counter and watched Tess layer thin cheese and tomato slices over the crushed herbs and sea salt she'd sprinkled on the bread. "Although we both figure you know what you're doing. If anyone knows how to handle a challenging professional relationship with a complicated, attractive man, it's you."

"Nothing like a little pressure."

Charlie grinned. "What are friends for?"

Hardy raced around the side of the house, barking with his stranger-near-the-gate voice. Seconds after, Jack strode inside and grabbed the platter heaped with steaks. "According to the alarm dog, our other guest has arrived," he said on his way back toward the patio. "I'll get these started and be right in."

"I'd better get the door," Charlie said.

"Wait." Tess pushed the baking sheet into her hands. "Stick this under the broiler and set the timer for a couple of minutes. Then go see if Jack needs any help outside."

"What are you up to?"

"I'm going to handle the uncomplicated social duties and answer the door."

Tess smiled as she passed through the high-wainscoted dining room, noticing Charlie's attempts to improve her surroundings. The antique oak table looked fairly presentable tonight, set with china instead of the usual paper plates. The front room's walls had been freshened with a pretty sage green and the windows hung with new tab curtains. A group of large throw pillows did their best to dress up the dull brown sofa.

Tess straightened the hem of her sweater, testing and rejecting a few snotty greetings as she neared the door. But then she remembered her intention to be charming, and she plastered a cordial expression on her face to hide her misgivings about the evening's possibilities.

As soon as she opened the door, her negative attitude evaporated. Quinn stood in the center of Charlie's tiny front porch, a bottle of wine in one hand and a grocery-stand bundle of pastel-blue irises in the other. He treated her to one of his long, penetrating looks, and she stared right back, noting the shower-damp hair curling at the ends, his freshly shaved jaw and a trace of some woodsy cologne. In his faded chamois shirt and worn leather jacket, he looked as sinfully delicious as a dark chocolate truffle with a buttercream center.

"You changed," she said.

"Not entirely." He edged past her, into the front room. "I'm still the same thorn in your side I've always been."

"The flowers are beautiful."

"They're not for you," he said when Tess reached for them.

"I figured." She gently pried the ribbony blooms from his grip. "I'll put these in water for Charlie. She's got her hands full." She glanced up at his shuttered expression. "Thoughtful of you."

He grunted in response.

"Hey, Quinn." Charlie walked into the room wearing

one of her sunny grins and wiping her hands on a dish towel. "Glad you could make it."

"Thanks for the invitation." He handed her the wine. "Stan Kessler recommended this."

"Then I'm sure it'll be great. Thanks." She studied the label. "I guess I'll go ahead and open this. Let it breathe awhile. We can have it with dinner."

"None for me," Quinn said. "Thanks, anyway."

"Okay. More for Jack and me." Charlie glanced at the stems in Tess's hands, and her grin widened. "Flowers?"

Quinn cleared his throat. "They're for you."

"Did Stan recommend these, too?" Tess asked sweetly. Charlie shot her a warning look.

"They're great." Charlie said. "Thanks, Quinn. What can I get you to drink?"

"Water."

"Ice?"

"Don't go to any trouble," he said.

"No trouble. I have to add it to Tess's, anyway."

"You're not having any wine?" Quinn asked Tess when Charlie had left the room.

"I rarely do. Long story."

Tess led him into the kitchen. Charlie handed him a glass and then pulled the bruschetta from the oven. "I'll be right back. Jack's nearly finished at the grill."

"Anything I can do to help?" Quinn asked.

"Got it under control, thanks." Charlie stepped outside.

Tess rummaged through Charlie's odds-and-ends drawer, looking for some scissors. "I hear you have a daughter," she mentioned casually. The statement was a legitimate conversation starter. Not an interrogation.

"Yeah."

"How old is she?"

"Ten."

Tess waited for him to offer more information, but it wasn't coming. She found a pair of shears and glanced around the room, wondering where Charlie kept her vases. No use spending too much time looking. Charlie probably didn't own a vase.

Tess searched the cupboards, hoping for a pitcher or a jar. "What's her name?"

"Rosie."

"Rosie Quinn. I like it." She discovered a fat ceramic mug and decided she could cut the stems shorter than usual for a compact bouquet. "Where is she tonight?" Tess asked in an offhand manner.

"With a friend."

Tess wondered if the friend was a classmate of his daughter's or a grown-up acquaintance of Quinn's, and then she decided she didn't really care. She didn't need to know all the details of his personal life in order to work with him. And she didn't like to snoop, not really. It wasn't her style.

She filled the mug with water and picked up one of the stems, gauging the best spot to make the cut. She'd merely been making an attempt at a casual conversation, using one of the oldest tricks in the social manual: getting the man to talk about himself. If he wouldn't cooperate, they wouldn't have a conversation.

Or they could have a conversation of a different kind. They could talk about her. Or she could choose a topic he'd be in a big hurry to change.

She turned with the flower in her hand and an overly bright smile on her face. "It looks like all that's left is the flower arranging. You can help with that…while we get to know each other better."

CHAPTER SEVEN

QUINN SLICED through one of the stems the way Tess had shown him while she fussed over the cut flowers in the mug and babbled about Charlie's upcoming wedding. He had a suspicion she was going on about flowers and cake and other girl-talk just to give him some grief, but he wasn't sure why. Not this time.

She usually gave him grief because he wasn't the one she'd wanted working with her on Tidewaters. That was too damn bad, because he wasn't going away. He thought they'd make a good team, if she could ever manage to pull that length of rebar out of her butt.

Until then, he'd just have to shut up, wait her out and get his part of the job done.

"Are you from around here?" she asked in another sudden shift in topic.

"Yeah."

She gave him a look that let him know there'd soon be more grief headed his way, but then her mouth curved again in that creepy smile, the one she'd been wearing since he walked in the door.

"Were you born here, then?" she asked.

God. More small talk. The from-the-beginning stuff. He stared out the window and took another gulp of water, hoping the steaks would be ready soon. "Yeah."

"Fascinating."

"Yeah."

"I wasn't." She crammed the flowers into the fat mug and leaned back against the counter, facing him. "I was born in a circus wagon somewhere on the road between Budapest and Paris."

He glanced over at her, trying to ignore the witchy challenge in her eyes, wondering what had inspired that off-the-wall comment, while waiting to find out what crazy thing she'd say or do next. Hoping for a clue to her mood.

"Hell of a long stretch of road," he said at last.

"Not for us traveling circus performers."

He tried to remain motionless, but his mouth twitched at one corner. "This must be part of that long story you mentioned."

"Yeah," she said.

Jack entered with a platter held high, out of reach of the drooling black Lab at his heels. "Evenin', Quinn. Good to see you."

"Good to be here."

And it was. It was pleasant, for a change, to visit with grown-ups in an informal social setting. He returned Charlie's smile as she passed by with a bowl of potatoes, and he chatted with Jack about the day's pour, and he chuckled at the dog's attempts to beg without getting caught. And he ignored Tess while she made a fuss over placing the flowers precisely in the center of the big, round table.

The flowers did look good, though. Pretty, especially the way Tess had arranged them. Dinner looked good, too. Simple, mouthwatering food. Except for those fancy little tomatoey things on the snack-size pieces of bread. Those seemed like something Tess would come up with.

A few minutes later, with a steak on his plate and the conversation flowing comfortably around him, Quinn began to relax. The camaraderie of this group of old friends made it easy for him to fade into the background, where he preferred to be. And the fact that Charlie and Jack were keeping Tess on a short leash helped, too.

He glanced across the table at her, watching those long, lovely hands gesture and her expressive eyes darken as she argued with Jack about Little League snack-shack politics. Vibrant and passionate, she was the kind of woman who liked a lot of drama in her life. The kind of woman who could wear a man out, in bed and out of it. Quinn sure didn't need any more drama in his life, but damn, a taste of Tess might be worth the exhaustion.

He wondered if he'd get a chance to ask her about her childhood circus experiences. He was looking forward to it.

"Here, Quinn." Jack offered a second serving of salad and then helped himself to another scoop. "You know, I was surprised it took Geneva as long as it did to get the city council to grant her Tidewaters permit."

"There's been a history of opposition to any development along the waterfront." Tess shrugged. "It's a handy location to spotlight. An easy focal point for the anti-growth crowd to use to drum up support for their cause."

"This particular project sure has people worked up." Jack paused to sip some wine. "I can see why they're concerned. It's a pretty spot."

"I may never be able to convince the people who prefer a patch of grass to a stretch of pavement that a new building can be a good thing." Tess twisted the stem of her water glass. "But I happen to think my design is an improvement on that vacant, weed-filled lot."

Jack nodded. "It is indeed."

"And when it's finished," Tess continued, "it'll generate plenty of tax revenue for the community."

"You know I agreed with all your arguments," Jack told her with one of his easy grins.

"I think the best thing about the design," Charlie said, "is that it won't compete with the surrounding buildings or setting. It'll fit right in. Look like it was meant to be there, all along."

"It'll look better than that." Quinn cleared his throat as the others at the table looked in his direction. "It'll be the most beautiful building in Carnelian Cove. Tess is going to be buried with work once people see what she can do."

He'd been staring at her as he spoke, so he'd seen her hands sink to her lap and her cheeks turn pink with a surprising and endearing blush. She opened her mouth as if she were about to say something, and then she grabbed her water glass and took a deep sip.

"You're right," Jack said. "It's a clever design, as Tess has reminded us plenty of times," he added with a wink. "An asset to the waterfront."

"Still," Charlie said, frowning, "some people are pretty worked up about it. I thought once the construction started, the letters to the editor would stop appearing in *The Cove Press*. I hope you won't have any problems."

"Any more problems, anyway," Jack said.

"I don't want any." Quinn waited for Tess's eyes to meet his. "That's why I'm taking precautions."

"The fence?" she asked.

"It's a start." He picked up his fork and poked at his salad. "I don't usually bother fencing in my sites."

"You told me that was for insurance purposes."

"There's all kinds of insurance," Quinn said as he glanced around the table. "And all kinds of trouble."

TESS DROVE to the job site after dinner. The conversation at the table had worried her, and she wouldn't be able to relax and fall asleep tonight unless she checked things out for herself.

A set of high-rise headlights settled behind her as she made the final turn toward the waterfront, and the deep rumble of a big truck's engine closed in on her roadster as she pulled to the curb. Quinn. Of course.

She scooted out of her car and started toward the silvery fence, carefully picking her way over uneven ground outlined in moonlight and pockmarked with shadow. A few seconds later, the thin beam of a flashlight swept across her path.

"You're going to twist your ankle," Quinn said from behind her.

"I can see just fine in the dark," Tess said, although the beam was a definite improvement.

"Like a cat."

"Meow."

He unlocked the gate, and they passed through. She let him take her elbow as they continued in silence toward the water's edge. Tidal ripples lapped at water-blackened rocks, and a ship's bell clanged somewhere near the marina. The odors of rotting seaweed trapped against the pilings and beef chargrilled at the nearby steak house hung in the shreds of bayside mist.

"It's getting late." Quinn bent to pick up a jagged scrap of lumber and tossed it toward his trailer. "We'd better go."

She pulled her outer sweater more snugly across her middle. "Why did you come out here?"

"I figured you'd head this way."

"What is this—some kind of game with you?" She turned toward him, but he faced the bay, his features obscured by evening shadows. "No matter when I drive by, you're always here. I never get a chance to—"

"To sit and imagine how it will be?"

"That's right."

He slid his hands into his pockets and nudged a loose stone. "To take a few moments at the beginning of what you know will be a long, hard day. Or to sneak a few moments before you have to leave at the end of it, setting aside all the frustrations. To have a few moments for yourself. Just you and the project."

He shifted in her direction, and she knew, without being able to see it, the precise expression he wore on his face. "To live in this place in a way no one else ever will," he said. "To see it in a way no one else can."

The damp night air tossed her bangs across her forehead, and in spite of her warm sweater, she shivered. She'd never heard him string so many words together before, and his eloquence—and his perception of what was inside her—caught her off guard. She didn't know how she could possibly share these thoughts and feelings with such a rough-edged, closed-off man. She'd never felt more uncomfortable with him than at this very second, when she realized how much they might have in common.

And she'd never before craved his approval with such an overwhelming longing. She supposed a large part of her resentment was tied up in that—in her need for his appreciation of her talents, in her desire for his acknowledgment of her importance to this project. He wouldn't be building Tidewaters without her vision.

"What do you see, when you look?" she asked.

"The angles of the walls. The glass in the panes. People moving along the walk, going into the shops. A nice tree somewhere along that curved drive you insist on having."

She smiled at his mention of the tree. And at the thought of the people who'd use the space—odd that she'd never pictured them in her daydreams. Now that she did, the image warmed her. "Some colorful planter boxes in front of the windows would be nice."

"Yeah. If they're like yours."

"Why, Quinn, how sweet." She raised her hand to brush her hair from her eyes. "I didn't think you'd noticed."

He circled her wrist with his strong, rough fingers and slowly guided her hand from her face. He'd never touched her before; she'd never imagined his first touch would be one like this, oddly gentle and tentative. She thought, for an instant—no, she hoped he'd continue the soft pressure, continue to pull her toward him until their bodies touched. She imagined the feel of him against her, solid and steady and male, and oh, my, a part of her wanted that, so very much.

But the desire, the insistent, warm beat inside her, reminded her of her lingering resentments—wanting him, and knowing he wanted her, and dealing with the fact that he could control or ignore these same urges, this shared awareness.

"I notice plenty," he said as he held her awkwardly in place, his voice a low rumble that seemed to set off vibrations as it moved through her. And then he dropped her hand and took her by the arm again.

"Time to go back," he said as he led her away. "It's safer here in the daylight."

THE DAWN FOG floated across dark bay ripples Monday morning to shroud the construction site in a ghostly haze. Quinn lugged a bundle of rebar toward the masonry wall rising above the second-floor level as Ned climbed the scaffolding to begin placing another stack of blocks. In the two weeks since the foundation had been poured, they'd forged ahead of schedule. Good thing, too, because a storm was forecast for the end of the week. In spite of the delay the rainy May weather would bring, he figured they'd still manage to have the south wall finished by this time next week, and the west wall framed and ready for—

An ominous crack echoed like gunfire across the bay, followed an instant later by a man's high-pitched yowl of panic and pain.

"Watch out!" Tom scrambled past the mortar mixer and dived beneath the planking as concrete blocks and a bright yellow hard hat tumbled to the muddy ground behind him.

Quinn dropped his load and raced toward the scaffolding. *No.* Not again. Not another man down. Not another nightmare ready to suck him down, too.

Rusty and Phil beat him to the ladder, clambering up to the spot where Ned lay, sprawled across two thick planks spanning the iron supports, cursing and panting and gripping a rail. Ned's legs dangled through the space where a third plank should have been. Rusty locked an arm over the scaffolding, bracing himself before he grabbed hold of Ned's belt to keep him from slipping over the edge.

"Hold still," Quinn ordered. He'd already flipped open his cell phone and punched a direct-dial number for emergency dispatch. *Come on, answer, damn it.*

"Don't worry." Ned cut off a groan with a grimace, his chest heaving. "I'm not going anywhere."

"What happened?" Tom swung up on the opposite edge.

"Board snapped." Ned muttered a curse, his face white with strain. "I grabbed for the rail and hit the edge on the way down. Think my leg's broke." He gasped. "Maybe a couple of ribs."

Quinn gave the emergency dispatcher their location and told her to send an ambulance. "Did you see what happened?" he asked as he flipped the phone shut.

Phil shook his head. "I was strapping on my tool belt. Next thing I knew, Tom was yelling, and I took off running."

"I heard the snap and saw the boards come down." Rusty glanced at the rest of them. "I thought for sure Ned was going to come down with 'em."

Quinn knelt beside Ned. Near the far side of the marina, a siren's keening horn cut through the smothering mist, momentarily blotting out Ned's short, heavy pants. "Think you can roll over a bit? We can try sliding in another plank to support you until help arrives."

"Sounds like a plan." With Rusty's help, Ned eased onto his back with a low grunt.

A fire truck lumbered through the gate and jerked to a stop beside the scaffolding. Emergency supplies in hand, a paramedic swung down and jogged toward the ladder.

"Let's give this guy some room," Quinn said. "Tom, wash out the mixer. Phil, go ahead and start in on the rebar on the west side. Rusty, call Gus at Keene's and see if you can get him to postpone the plaster sand delivery."

Quinn had a tougher call to make—one to Ned's wife, Sylvie—as soon as he got the chance.

His crew moved off as an ambulance pulled into the site. Behind the white cab, a dark green compact darted into view.

"Damn," Quinn muttered when the compact stopped at the curb beyond the fencing. Justin Gregorio, reporter for Channel Six news. No fan of development in general or Tidewaters in particular.

Or Quinn, for that matter. None of the men who'd dated Quinn's ex-wife before she'd left town had a very high opinion of him.

Which evened things out, since the lack of esteem was mutual.

Gregorio pulled a video camera from his car and panned the site, pausing when the lens swung in Quinn's direction. He slowly lowered the camera, a coldly false smile pasted on his face, and then he turned to wave at Rusty, who was stepping out of the office trailer.

With Quinn's help, the firemen lowered Ned's stretcher to the waiting gurney. The paramedic asked a few routine questions before loading Ned into the back of the ambulance, and then the van rolled across the site.

Quinn pulled out his phone, figuring he couldn't put off that call to Sylvie any longer. When she didn't answer, he left a message and tucked his phone in his pocket as Rusty approached. "What did Gus say?"

"Told him what happened. He said to give him a call around eleven, and he'd see what he could do. Probably won't be able to send a truck until after lunch."

"Okay. Thanks."

A police cruiser passed through the gate and headed toward the firemen chatting with Gregorio.

"Shit," Rusty said as he folded a fresh piece of gum into his mouth. "It's like Grand Central Station around here."

Quinn stared across the yard. "I saw you talking to the guy from Channel Six.

"Yeah." Rusty tugged on his work gloves. "He sure was looking to dig up some trouble. I don't think he found enough to suit him."

"Thanks. Again."

Quinn sent him to join Phil and then strolled toward the cruiser. "Morning, Reed."

"Morning." Reed Oberman tilted his chin toward the walkie-talkie on his shoulder and mumbled a cop's code of numbers and acronyms into it. "Heard you had some trouble down here."

"All taken care of."

"So it seems."

"Hey, Reed." Gregorio edged his way into the conversation and extended a hand. "Good to see you."

"Is that off the record?"

Gregorio flashed a bland smile at the officer and then faced Quinn. "Morning, Quinn. Shame to hear you're having trouble on your job sites again. Looks like another innocent member of your crew's hurt, and no one knows why."

"No comment," Quinn said.

"No comment on a friendly expression of sympathy?" Gregorio's smile widened. "That seems a bit extreme. Damn near defensive, considering the circumstances."

"No comment."

"How about you, Reed? Are you here in an official capacity?"

"You know city policy on emergency dispatch." Behind them, Reed's car radio crackled and squawked. "And my business here is private. Unless Quinn doesn't mind?"

Quinn flicked a glance in Gregorio's direction. "No comment."

"In that case," Reed said with a tight smile of his own for Gregorio, "I'm going to have to ask you to stand back."

"No problem," Gregorio said. "Catch you later, Quinn."

"No comment," Quinn said.

Gregorio hefted his camera to his shoulder and moved off toward the scaffold.

"You want me to remove him from the site?" Reed asked.

"No. Thanks." Quinn gestured toward his trailer. "Coffee? I don't have anything but black, but it's hot."

"No, thanks. I'm cutting back." Reed pulled a notepad from his pocket. "What happened here this morning, Quinn?"

In terse, precise phrases, Quinn went over everything he'd seen and everything he'd learned. "I don't know why that board snapped the way it did," he finished. "But I'm going to find out."

"Sounds like an accident to me."

"Looks like it. But it's not." Quinn watched Gregorio duck into his little green car. "I checked every one of those boards and put them in place myself."

Reed glanced up from his notetaking, his expression cool, professional and shuttered.

CHAPTER EIGHT

BECAUSE they were beginning to shake, Quinn buried his hands in his pockets and swallowed the acrid taste of panic. He knew what Reed was thinking—what everyone in town would be thinking, once Gregorio reminded them of what had happened on one of Quinn's job sites six years ago. A member of his crew had fallen and broken his back.

"Sounds like Ned was lucky." Reed folded the flap on his notebook and slipped it into his pocket.

"Or unlucky enough to be in the wrong place at the wrong time." Quinn turned and started toward the blocks scattered around the mixer. "Let's have a look."

Reed followed him beneath the scaffold. Quinn tugged one of the broken boards from its awkward angle on the cross-bracing and studied the twisted, ragged edge. Then he flipped it over and found a fresh, neat slice below the jagged slivers. His fingers tightened on the wood, his knuckles whitening as he squeezed, remembering the gut-icing snap and Ned's scream.

Reed leaned in closer for a better look. "That looks too clean to be an accidental break."

"That's because this was no accident." Quinn shifted his grip and traced the smooth cut. "This board's been sawed more than three-quarters through. From the top side, no one would have noticed anything was wrong until—"

"Until he stepped on that spot and broke it the rest of the way." Reed pulled out his pad and scribbled more notes. "Mind if I take that into evidence? Just in case you get a chance to press charges."

"Be my guest." Quinn yanked the other half of the board from under the pile of blocks and layered it over the first. The two sections weren't going to fit into Reed's patrol car. "Want me to put these in my truck and follow you to the station?"

"That won't be necessary." Reed's radio squawked to life, and he spoke into his shoulder set. "I'll send for some assistance," he said when he was finished. "I'd like to talk to the rest of your crew before I go."

Quinn waved him off and headed for his trailer. He wanted some time to simmer down, to cool off before he called Sylvie. In fact, he wanted to shut down for the day, to swing by the hospital to check on Ned, but he couldn't. He couldn't run. He had to stick it out, to stay focused. To battle back the urge to detour to the nearest liquor store and wrap his fingers around the comforting, promising weight of a thick, cool bottle. To raise it to his lips, to let the liquid heat slide down his throat and smooth out the shakes, to lose himself in the—

He jogged up the steps, slammed the door and tossed his hat onto the short counter with a curse, and then he pressed the heels of his hands against his eyes. *No.* There was Rosie, and Ned, and the crew, and this job. The building, rising from the ground.

He lowered his arms and stared through the filmy, fly-specked window at the stark beauty of the I-beams rising from the foundation and the clean sweep of the yard.

The power, the potential in this new start. He had to stick around, stay on track, keep moving. Moving forward.

He paced a tight circle, sucking in one shallow, wavering breath after another and blowing it out. Another set of slower, deeper breaths, and yet another, until each silent sigh carved away a part of the gnawing, crippling need, and Quinn knew he'd be fine…for another five minutes or so.

Five minutes would buy him enough time to make a start on the next hour. And that hour would be the down payment on the next one after that.

God. He'd hoped that because he'd been able to pull himself out of the last panic attack—the one following the damage to the backhoe—he'd be better able to handle the stress on the job. But the vandalized equipment hadn't hit him this hard. Because of Ned, because of…what had happened six years ago.

Because this morning's act of vandalism seemed personal.

Would this ever get easier? Would he ever be able to make a break with his past? The despair nearly sucked him under again, and he lifted his gaze to the picture of Rosie pinned to the bulletin board above the counter.

Rosie. Counting on him.

He leaned a shoulder against the wall, as fragile and worn as a thousand-year-old parchment, fumbling in his pocket for the cell phone with fingers that no longer seemed to hold the strength to shake. There were two more calls he needed to make this morning. One to Geneva and one to Tess.

He'd phone Tess first. His mouth quirked up in one corner, and a thin layer of misery evaporated as he thought about how hot she'd get if he didn't report in on time. And about how appealing she looked when she was throwing one of her subtly steamy tantrums.

Through the window, he watched Gregorio lift his camera to get a shot of the scaffolding, and a fresh wave of anger bubbled through him. Clean, healthy, energizing anger. No, he wouldn't leave his site. Not yet. Not with the newsman prowling around, poking through the remains of this day's disaster and looking for an angle on the wreckage of the past.

TESS STRODE through the entry of Cove Community Medical Center shortly after her lunch meeting on Monday afternoon. This was the first chance she'd had to break away and check on things—on Ned—for herself. Anger and worry were doing unpleasant things to the Greek salad with extra feta cheese she'd ordered at Café Capri, where a potential client had begun the business discussion by asking about the latest trouble at Tidewaters.

Which had been about five minutes before Geneva had reached her on her cell phone, wanting the same information. Obviously, the news about Ned's accident had already spread through town. And just as obviously, Quinn hadn't been able to reach Geneva before she'd heard the rumors. Tess rubbed a hand over her stomach and wondered if she'd ever order extra feta again.

She rounded a corner and nearly collided with Quinn, who was standing near the elevator, a large bouquet of yellow daisy mums in one hand. Their slightly sweet scent mingled with the odor of disinfectant in a typical hospital smell, making her slightly queasy.

"Flowers again?" she asked as she nervously punched a button that was already lit. "For Ned?"

"For Sylvie." The plastic wrap crackled as he tightened his grip on the bouquet. "For having to put up with Ned at home for a while."

Quinn's lips were pressed flat, his grim face deeply lined. He looked as though he'd aged ten years since she'd last seen him.

"How did he fall through the scaffolding?" she asked.

"He didn't fall clear through." The elevator doors slid open, and they stepped aside as an attendant exited, wheeling a supply cart past them.

"So," she said, "he only fell far enough to end up here."

Quinn slapped a hand against the side of the opening and waited for her to step into the elevator ahead of him. "You can ask him exactly how far he fell and exactly how bad he's hurt when you see him."

She opened her mouth to respond, but a snappy, snotty comeback didn't materialize as quickly as she'd hoped. Just as well—this wasn't the time or the place for that kind of remark. She adjusted the purse strap on her shoulder, fixed her gaze on the control panel and focused on resenting the way the stiff and silent man beside her could scramble her normal reactions and put her on the defensive.

They stepped off the elevator and headed toward the nurses' station in the outpatient wing. A petite, doe-eyed blonde in a blue waitress uniform and rubbery white shoes rose from a nearby chair and walked into the arms Quinn had spread wide. He wrapped her tight, resting his chin on her wavy hair. "Sorry about all this," he murmured.

"Couldn't be helped." She eased back, her smile wavering. "He's always been a clumsy oaf."

"Clumsy had nothing to do with it." Quinn shot Tess a dark look over the woman's head.

"Bad luck, then." She stepped out of his arms and looked questioningly at Tess.

"Sylvie Landreau, this is Tess Roussel. The architect who designed the Tidewaters project."

Tess extended her hand. "Sorry to be meeting you under these circumstances, Sylvie. I hope your husband will recover quickly and be back to work soon."

"Me, too. Especially the back-to-work part." Sylvie accepted the flowers Quinn handed her and wiped a finger beneath one of her eyes. "He's already grouchy as a bear. I came out here for some peace."

"Is there anything I can do?" Quinn asked. "Pick up something at the drugstore? Get a takeout dinner for you and the kids?"

Sylvie shook her head. "Thanks, but Mom is coming to help out tonight. I'm thinking of asking her to move in for a while. That ought to cut Ned's recovery time in half."

She shifted to the side as an orderly wheeled a chair past them and into a nearby room. "That must be for Ned. I'd better go."

"Geneva called," Tess said when Sylvie had disappeared into a room down the hall. "She wants us to meet with her at Chandler House. This afternoon, if possible."

"No."

"Tonight, then."

"I'll give her a call when I have something new to report."

"You've got plenty to report right now," Tess said. "You can start by filling me in on all those details you didn't have time to discuss with me when you called this morning."

He glanced down the hall toward Ned's room. "Later. I've got to get back to work."

"Fine. I'll follow you to the site, and we can have our meeting in your trailer. In about…" She made a show of checking her watch. "Fifteen minutes. Is that 'later' enough for you?"

He leveled a stony gaze at her while a little muscle in his jaw popped. Then he took her by the arm and led her down the hall, away from the small crowd of hospital employees hovering near the nurses' station.

"Someone cut through that plank," he said in a tight, low voice. "The one that gave way when Ned stepped on it."

"On the scaffolding?" Her fingers trembled as she fussed with her purse strap. "How can you be sure?"

He shifted aside as a nurse passed, and then he waited until she disappeared into one of the rooms. "I saw the cut. Fresh, and made with a saw. Nearly clean through, on one side, and underneath, where you wouldn't see it."

"Wasn't the planking checked when the scaffolding was erected?"

Quinn's eyes iced over, and she could nearly see the anger pumping off him to vibrate in the air around them. "I checked it."

Before Tess could ask another question, the orderly wheeled Ned into the hall. Sylvie trailed behind, carrying the flowers and a messy handful of medical paperwork. Quinn moved off to join them on their trip toward the elevator doors, leaving Tess frozen in place, trying to process what Quinn had just told her.

Sabotage. Deliberate, and intended to cause someone a serious injury. Or worse.

Chilled through and shaking, she drew in a deep breath, donned a bright smile and walked toward the Landreaus, preparing to offer her sincere sympathies.

She'd grown fond of Quinn's crew, and this morning's accident had upset her a great deal, far more than Quinn would ever suspect. And now that she knew the reason for Ned's injury, her anxiety increased. What might happen next?

"Hey, Tess," Ned said as she approached. "I don't think I've ever seen you without a bakery bag in your hand."

She kept her eyes on his face, avoiding the ungainly, pale cast on his leg. "Tell me what you like, and I'll make a special trip to Bern's Bakery just for you."

"You don't have to, you know," Sylvie said. "Although we appreciate the thought."

"It's not just a thought." Ned smiled up at Tess. "It's a bright spot in the day when Tess here shows up with something sweet."

"In that case," Sylvie said with a shy smile of her own, "Marie-Claudette's molasses cookies are a favorite at our house."

"Molasses cookies, then. It's a deal." Tess stepped into the open elevator with the others and then rested her hand on Ned's shoulder. "Sorry you had to go through all this to get a home delivery."

"I'd have preferred to skip it, myself." He gave Quinn a long, level look. "But I'll be back as soon as I can."

"I'm counting on it."

When they left the elevator on the ground floor, Quinn pulled Sylvie into another quick, tight hug while the orderly wheeled Ned toward the hospital entrance. "Call me if you need anything," he said. "Anything at all."

Sylvie nodded. "Thanks, Quinn." She waved good-bye to Tess and jogged through the lobby to join her husband.

"Why would someone do that?" Tess asked as the

Landreaus moved through the big glass doors and out into the afternoon sunshine. Ned said something to Sylvie and reached for her hand, and she laughed as she slid her fingers through his. "Why would someone want to hurt—maybe even kill—a total stranger like that?"

Quinn shoved his hands into his pockets. "Maybe the target wasn't a stranger."

Another icy tremor slicked down her back. "That's a frightening accusation to make. Who could have wanted to hurt Ned, specifically? Or any one of your crew members who might have stepped on that piece of scaffolding?"

"That's what I'd like to know."

He started across the lobby, and she lengthened her stride to catch up. "You need to talk to Geneva," she said.

"I told you I would."

"About what you just told me."

"I intend to."

She reached the door before he did and turned to face him, blocking his path. "I'd like to be there when you do."

He stared at her, his eyes narrowed, considering. "What time does she want to meet with me?"

"Six o'clock."

"All right. I'll be there." The tiny muscles of his jaw rippled again and then smoothed in a rigid cast. "I have a few questions of my own."

CHAPTER NINE

TESS SHIFTED her roadster into a lower gear and roared through the wide gate of Chandler House ten minutes after six o'clock. Why had she ever agreed to such a ridiculous meeting time, she asked herself as she jolted to a stop beneath the porte cochere. Right in the middle of the dinner hour. She hadn't had time to change out of the summery block-print dress and patent leather heels she'd worn to work that day. She'd barely had time to drink the soothing miso soup she'd picked up at Kamakura on the way home, and she'd had to stuff her sushi in her refrigerator for later. Stale sushi—ugh.

Oh, well. It wasn't as if she'd have been able to eat the fussy, spicy food anyway, not with her skittery stomach. Not after what Quinn had told her at the hospital. And not after the shame and guilt that had drifted in and settled over her, smothering her appetite and scattering her thoughts.

She'd panicked that afternoon. She'd left the hospital and returned to her office, locked the door, turned off the lights and hidden in the late-afternoon shadows behind her desk, resting her head in her hands while aftershocks rattled through her. Her brilliant, lovely Tidewaters. Geneva's hopes and all their plans, splintering at the edges. Ned, laid up and in pain, and sweet Sylvie left to deal with the aftermath.

And Quinn… Well. She couldn't begin to imagine how this was affecting him. She didn't want to think about it.

No, she hadn't devoted much time to thinking about what Tidewaters meant to anyone else or how it might impact their lives. She'd been so wrapped up in her own design and ambitions, in Geneva's goals and vision, that she hadn't looked beyond the foundation and walls and connective tissue of the building to see the others involved in bringing it to life.

By the time she braked to a stop at the side entry and grabbed a light sweater before hopping out of her car, she was finished with doubt and self-recrimination. It was time to turn her energy to something more productive than beating up on herself. Time to take the fight to someone else.

What was going on? What did Quinn suspect? She'd learned that so-called journalist from Channel Six had been snooping around the site. Maybe that's why Geneva had chosen this meeting time, so they could all watch Justin Gregorio's newscast together.

Although Tess was much more interested in hearing Quinn's version of the events.

She slipped through the side entrance and started down the back hall, but made a quick detour into the kitchen when she heard a pot clang against a countertop. "Hi there, Julia."

"Hi there yourself, young lady." Julia swung the faucet over the kettle she was holding and began to fill it with water. "Your grandmama's in the second parlor, waiting for you."

"Thanks." Tess tortured herself with an extravagant sniff of the aroma wafting from the oven. "Is Quinn here yet?"

"Right on time." Julia cast a pointed look over her shoulder. "Unlike some other people I could mention."

"Nag, nag, nag. It's a wonder I put up with you." Tess darted in close to give the cook a smacking kiss on her cheek. "Are those your almond cookies I smell?"

"Could be."

"Are some of them for me?"

"Could be." Julia elbowed Tess aside and carried the kettle to the cooktop. "If you get out of here and let me finish what I'm doing."

Tess moved back into the dim hallway. She could hear Geneva's questioning tone and Quinn's low, steady rumble as she neared the blue parlor, the one Geneva used as a casual, private space—the only room on the ground floor with a television. She faltered for a moment, pressing a fist against her stomach. And then she pasted a bright smile on her face and struck a relaxed pose in the doorway. "I hope you haven't started without me."

"You're late." Geneva smoothed a hand over the Yorkie perched in her lap. She was seated in her favorite high-backed chair, a throne upholstered in blue-and-white toile. Tess had always associated toile with formality and ultimatums.

"Yes, I'm late. As usual," she said with an overplayed sigh. "My one and only vice."

She sauntered into the room, dropped her purse on the floor, draped her sweater over one arm of a sofa and settled on the soft, deep cushion beside them. "Hello, Quinn."

From the opposite end of the sofa, he grunted a masculine greeting. He lounged against the corner pillows, his legs extending in two long, lean, jean-clad lines and his boots crossed and stacked on the plush rug. He'd managed to change from his grubby work clothes into cleaner jeans, and he wore his standard leather jacket over a blue shirt that matched the color of his eyes. No time to shave, though—dark stubble edged his jaw, giving him a slightly rough and dangerous cast.

Geneva lifted a remote and aimed it at the television as Justin's face appeared on the screen, increasing the volume until his deep, smooth voice filled the room. "City police were called to the scene early this morning at Tidewaters, the construction site adjoining the bay at the intersection of Front Street and Clipper Road in Carnelian Cove. This was the second visit in less than a month that the police have made to this controversial building project."

"Controversial," Tess muttered in disgust as she crossed her arms. Geneva held up her hand, signaling for silence.

The scene shifted to a nervous-looking Rusty speaking into Justin's microphone. "I heard a sn—a loud snap, and then Ned…he must have slipped through the hole in the scaffolding."

Justin tilted the microphone toward his own chin. "Who was it that put that particular piece of the scaffolding in place?"

"I-I'm not sure," Rusty said, seeming more uncomfortable by the moment.

"You're not in charge of the scaffolding?"

"No." Rusty relaxed, obviously relieved he could answer a question without having to worry about his phrasing. "That's Quinn."

Justin appeared in a new shot, strolling along one of the docks on the marina. "That's J. J. Quinn, the general contractor chosen to build Tidewaters. It's interesting to note the similarities between today's accident, involving a construction worker's fall through a faulty piece of scaffolding, with an incident on another of Quinn's construction projects just a few years ago, when one of his crew members plummeted from the scaffolding and broke his back."

Julia stepped through the door with a coffee-and-dessert tray and paused to watch the television.

"Today the worker on Quinn's site was luckier," continued Justin, "suffering only a broken leg and some badly bruised ribs. But police are investigating the scene."

"That rat," Tess said. "He made it sound as though—"

Suddenly, Howard Cobb appeared on the screen, speaking into Justin's microphone from a different marina location. "I warned the city that there were numerous problems associated with the Tidewaters project, but I never expected this kind of trouble. I guess today's incident is just one example...." He broke off, appearing to consider his next words with great care. "It seems to furnish proof that those of us who opposed the building...well, we had our reasons for doing so."

Justin turned to face the camera, the waters of the bay behind him. "We tried to reach Tidewaters' developer, Geneva Chandler, for a comment, but she declined to speak with Channel Six news. We can only hope that her construction project won't continue to be plagued with bad luck. For Channel Six news, this is Justin Gregorio in Carnelian Cove."

GENEVA PRESSED a button on the remote to switch off the television. Too bad she couldn't do the same with the nasty campaign waged by Howard Cobb and his accomplices in the media. "Cleverly done," she said. "I'm quite impressed. And I didn't think that was possible."

"Oh, it was clever, all right." Tess pushed out of her seat to pace the room restlessly. "What an outrageous, slimy pack of innuendoes and outright— Arghh!"

"Makes me feel dirty just listening in," Julia muttered as she set the tray on a table near Geneva's chair.

"I have to agree with you both," Geneva said as she smiled and nodded her thanks to Julia. "Although I'm not sure which slimy thing or person you're referring to."

"Does it matter?" Julia straightened and brushed her hands over her apron. "If you'll carry this tray into the kitchen when everyone's finished, Miss Tess, I'll deal with it in the morning."

"That's fine," Geneva said. "Thank you, Julia. I'll see you tomorrow."

Tess folded her arms, lifted one hand to her mouth and began to chew the side of her thumb in a nervous childhood habit Geneva had thought she'd cured. "I'm glad you didn't talk to that Gregorio creep," Tess said. "He'd have found some way to mess it up."

"Which is precisely why I declined his invitation." Geneva lifted the coffeepot and one of the cups. "Coffee, Quinn?"

"Sure. Thanks." He stood and took the cup Geneva offered and then moved across the room to stare through the window facing the ocean.

"And why is Howard Cobb sticking his hairy, bulbous nose into any of this?" Tess paused in her pacing to grab two cookies from the plate. "He had the good sense to recuse himself from the council votes on the permit process. Why is he talking to the news now?"

"He may be reconsidering the wisdom of investing so much in the development of his commercial park along the river." Geneva lifted a dessert plate and napkin for Tess to take when she passed by again. "There aren't all that many professionals needing office space in Carnelian Cove, and Tidewaters will be stiff competition for him."

"He should have seen this coming when you started the permit process on Tidewaters." Tess bit into one of the cookies. "He should have known he might have trouble finding enough tenants to fill his building."

"He thought he could stop me." Geneva's lips twisted in a tiny smile. "He should have known better about that, too."

She stirred a bit of cream into the coffee she'd poured for herself. Quinn stood utterly still at the window, his back to the rest of the room. A quiet, curious man. Steady and resolute, in spite of his past shortcomings— or perhaps because of them. Geneva suspected his brooding appearance sometimes masked an impatience with the dramas swirling around him.

Time to draw him into this one. "I am concerned, however," she said, "about the points Mr. Gregorio made about the curious history of problems Quinn has had on his construction sites. I wouldn't want those problems tainting Tidewaters' reputation before it's completed."

"That's not fair." Tess dropped her cookie on her plate. "Anything that happened before has nothing to do with this. The first 'problem' Gregorio mentioned at Tidewaters was a random act of vandalism. And Quinn told me the second problem wasn't an accident at all— that board had been cut."

Geneva gave her a long, bland look. "And do you believe everything that Quinn tells you?"

"Of course I do." Tess's plate clattered as she set it on the tea table. The second cookie—one of Tess's favorites—was still untouched. "Why wouldn't I?"

"Because of the specific types of problems he's had before on his job sites." Geneva sipped her coffee. "Because he has an alleged history of negligence."

"That's…that's ridiculous." Tess spun toward Quinn, who continued to stare out the window. "Isn't it? Quinn?"

"I'm sure you've heard the rumors, too," Geneva said quietly.

"Gossip." Tess resumed her pacing. "He hasn't been negligent, not one bit. Hell, I haven't been able to find five minutes to enjoy that site for myself since—"

She turned slowly, suspicion evident in her expression. "You wouldn't have hired him if you'd had any doubts."

"It was your doubts that most concerned me." Geneva finished her coffee and set her cup aside. "I'm relieved to see you seem to have resolved them."

"Don't you have anything to say?" Tess strode across the room toward the spot where Quinn remained, silent and impassive. "Are you just going to stand there and not say a word about any of this?"

"You were doing enough talking for both of us."

He turned his head, and his features seemed to soften as he gazed at Tess. A quick, shadowy creasing around his eyes, a momentary twist of his lips. But his expression hardened as he moved to face Geneva. "The only thing I want to know," he said, "is whether you think Cobb had anything to do with the vandalism. Or with the scaffolding—with hurting Ned."

"I'd like to say that I'm certain Howard would never arrange anything so stupid. Or dangerous." Geneva looked up at them both. "But I can't. He's a clever man, and an ambitious one, but he's done some incredibly foolish things."

"How can we find out?" Tess added several cookies

to her plate and sank back into her seat on the sofa. Crisis averted; appetite back in place. "If he's behind this, I want to nail his ass to the wall."

"Please, Tess. That statement is disturbing on so many levels." Geneva sighed and ran her fingers along the fold of the napkin still in her lap. "I suppose I could hire an investigator."

Quinn's frown deepened. "Isn't this police business?"

"The city police won't want to look in Howard's direction." Geneva leaned her head against the chair cushion, suddenly weary of the twists and turns this project had taken. She'd hoped that once construction had started, opposition to Tidewaters would fade. "An investigator will act on our suspicions," she added.

"And what if we're wrong?" asked Tess. "We might send him off on a wild-goose chase—an expensive one—while the real culprit gets away with it."

"There's something else an investigator could do." Quinn set his cup on the table. "He could keep an eye on the site. I can't be there twenty-four hours a day."

"And I'm not about to hire a bodyguard for a city block." Geneva laid her napkin on the tray. "I think we've exhausted this topic for the evening. I'm sure that after we've all had time to rest and consider matters from different perspectives, we'll be much better equipped to put a plan in motion."

She rose from her chair. "Is there anything else we need to discuss tonight?"

"Just one thing." Tess stood and brushed cookie crumbs from her dress skirt. "J. J. Quinn?"

The corners of Quinn's mouth lifted in the semblance of a grin. "Yeah. Stands for John Jameson."

"I never knew," Tess said.

"You never asked."

Tess gave him one of her sly, catlike smiles. "Guess it's time to start filling in the blanks."

Geneva hid a smile of her own at their teasing, feeling much less weary than she'd felt a short while ago.

CHAPTER TEN

TESS PASSED THROUGH the side porte cochere door Quinn opened for her and stepped onto a landing enveloped in ocean-scented fog. The damp air brushed over her skin, leaving a trail of goose bumps behind. She shivered as she thrust her arms through her sweater and pulled it tightly across her middle. "I am *so* ready for summer."

He didn't respond, and she knew he was simply standing there, staring at her in that intense, motionless way of his. Wishing he'd quit the unsettling habit or telling herself to ignore those gorgeous, black-lashed, deep-set blue eyes of his wouldn't reduce their effect on her nerves.

She glanced over her shoulder to find his tall, lean form framed by the massive door and backlit in the amber glow of twin carriage-house sconces. His gaze was as piercing as ever, but there was something new in his somber expression tonight. Something searching, something uncertain. It might have been the feeble lighting or the mist, but she thought she detected something…softer.

"What are you waiting for?" she asked. "Did you forget something?"

"No."

She paused, expecting some kind of explanation, but he continued to study her, as if by merely looking he could penetrate her pores and strip bare all her secrets. She shrugged off her fanciful thoughts and walked down the steps, headed toward her car.

"You could have had me fired," he said.

"Maybe." She reached for the handle and then turned to face him. She wanted to push back, to knock him off balance and make him feel as uneasy as he made her. "Probably."

He stepped down to the drive. "Why didn't you?"

"You're not worth the trouble."

He shifted closer, shaking his head. "I'm going to be more trouble if you keep me on the job."

"Is that a threat?"

His gaze roamed over her face, lingering on her mouth before raising to her eyes. His pupils expanded in the semidarkness until his eyes seemed as black as the pavement beyond the porch lights. "It wasn't intended as one."

"Well, then." She let out the breath she'd been holding and sucked in chilled air, but the tiny tremor that followed wasn't caused by the cold.

"It was a statement of fact," he said.

He'd moved again, and he was standing much closer. Too close. The arches of the porte cochere cast sharp shadows over his features, outlining his angular cheeks and lining the deep grooves around his mouth.

She tossed her head back, shaking her bangs out of her eyes before angling her face toward his. "I like a man who's honest about his bad intentions."

One side of his mouth tugged to the side in something that wasn't quite a grin. Something dangerous, something potent. "If I ever have any of those, I'll be sure to let you know."

"It's a deal."

He lifted a hand to her sweater and ran his fingertips from button to button, along the opening. His knuckles skimmed over her breast, and her nipples tightened and tingled.

"All right then," he said. And then he grew very still, as only he could do, and looked at her in that way that made everything in her aware of everything about him. Of his height, and his breadth, and his strength, and his ridiculous, impossible appeal.

His thumb moved over the soft sweater wool, back and forth, in a soft caress, and her pulse pounded in her ears. *Kiss me kiss me kiss me...*

His lashes lowered again, and her lips parted on a silent gasp.

"Good night," he said.

"Right." She reached behind her, grabbing for the car's handle with trembling fingers. "See you around."

He disappeared beyond the bend, and she collapsed in her seat and pulled her door closed. A minute later, the deep vibrations of a big truck's engine rumbled through the dark, and then the ghostly glare of headlights swept through the fog.

"Damn, that was a close call." She turned her key in the ignition and pressed the heat and fan buttons. Warm air flooded the compartment, and she closed her eyes and slumped in her seat to wait for her sanity to return. "Too close."

Too bad it hadn't been closer. Closer would have been damn good.

QUINN COASTED down the winding bluff road, braking around the tight, shadowed corners, keeping his eyes on the road and his thoughts on the week ahead. He could do without Ned for a few days, but he'd need to take on more help before the end of the month. He'd check on the fencing around the site and ask Reed about the possibility of having a patrol car pass by a couple of times a night.

Payroll was coming up again. And his call to the city inspector to visit the site and sign off on the rough plumbing had gone unanswered—time to step up the pressure on the building department. Better phone the mill yard while he was at it, double-check the delivery schedule for the framing material. And find some time to talk with Tess about the specs for those glue-lam beams.

Tess. His fingers tightened on the wheel as his thoughts detoured into forbidden paths and blurred with the mist around him. Bits of the conversation beneath Geneva's porch, that distorted slice of time before he'd made his escape. Those pulsing, electrifying moments when Tess's head had tilted back, her lids drifting low over her whiskey eyes, her lips moist and begging, her breath a warm zephyr on his face, her flower-garden scent battering his self-control.

Control. The one thing he wouldn't let her wrest from him, no matter how hard she tried. No matter how much he was tempted to surrender. If he took her up on her offer, it would be on his terms, not hers.

He'd been fighting this craving for weeks. Watching her, testing himself. Reasoning things through. She wasn't a chemical; she wasn't a drug. She wasn't any-thing addictive—she wasn't as insidious or dangerous as that. She wasn't anything he couldn't handle if he chose to try. He could walk away if he decided to. He'd done it before several times. The choice was up to him.

And he'd decided, by the time he'd descended from

the bluff and reached level ground, that he was tired of fighting something that wasn't a real threat, something that was bound to feel better than booze and more satisfying than tobacco. Why should he deprive himself—and Tess—of something that good? Sure, adding another layer to a complicated relationship might not be the best idea in the world. But she wanted this, too.

Is that an invitation?

Do you have to ask?

He slowed to a stop at an intersection near the marina and glanced at the headlights slung low across his rearview mirror. The headlights of a sassy red roadster. He'd known, before he pulled through Geneva's gate, that she'd follow him here. He'd seen the heat and the bafflement in her dark eyes, and he'd understood she couldn't leave things the way he'd left them. Unfinished, untidy. She liked things organized and beautifully arranged, and he liked that about her.

There were a great many things he liked about her, in spite of the pinprick twinges that came with admitting that fact. He knew he'd be safer if he continued viewing her as an irritant or an adversary, instead of…however it was he was beginning to think of her. He'd have to finish those thoughts, the sooner the better. And if they led to bad intentions, well, he'd have to let her know about those, just as he'd promised.

For now, he'd prefer to deal with whatever it was that was arcing between them tonight. He turned along the waterfront, pulled to a stop to unlock the gate, and then jounced about twenty yards into the Tidewaters site.

He stepped out of his truck and closed the door, waiting for the timed lights to switch off and plunge him into the uncertain darkness of the fog-draped, moonlit night. Waited for the low growl of Tess's roadster to click to a stop, for her to stretch one of her long legs to the ground as she exited. She'd worn a pair of those black, high-heeled shoes tonight, the ones with the lethal-looking points at the toes and the sexy curves along the heels. She'd wobble a bit as she crossed the gravel-lined yard, making her way toward him, but it wouldn't trip her up. She never lost her footing, no matter how tough the terrain.

Maybe he'd kiss her for the first time here, where they were on equal ground. Maybe he'd put his hands on her, sliding his fingers beneath the soft wool of her sweater and the thin straps of her pretty dress to skim them along her warm, womanly skin, with the silent bay as their slick, inky backdrop. Whenever he thought of her, the image was done up in tones of gray and black. Plenty of black, like the sweep of her hair and the suits she wore and the thin frames of the designs hanging on her office walls. Of the shadowy emotions she summoned from deep inside him.

Maybe she'd put her hands on him—those narrow, soft-looking palms, those long fingers with their slick, painted nails. He was getting hard thinking about it.

And chilled, standing here, anxious for her to get out of her car. He tucked his hands in his pockets and stared at the neon dots of streetlights reflected on her sloping windshield like a glittering constellation. Maybe she was thinking of what they'd say to each other before he pulled her into his arms. And what they'd say after he let her go.

He wasn't going to find out. The roadster roared away from the curb, raced down the street and swerved around the corner, heading into the heart of town.

She'd left him standing in the cold night air, waiting for her to make a move, thinking about kissing her.

"Damn." A guy had to admire a woman who could give as good as she got.

AFTER CHANNELING his frustrations into a long bout of paperwork in his lonely office trailer and making a stop at a twenty-four-hour grocery store, Quinn quietly let himself into his apartment. Rosie sat on the sofa beside a snoring Neva, the television remote in one hand and a murderous expression on her face. "Finally," she said.

He checked the clock on the book stand. Ten-fifteen. Over an hour past her bedtime. "Why are you still up?"

She flicked a glance at Neva. "Who's supposed to make me go to bed?"

"It's a school night. You know the rules."

"It's a work night, too. Guess you had a lot to do."

"Sorry I'm late. How long has Neva been asleep?" He carefully shifted the bag of groceries in his arms as he moved toward the kitchen, uneasy about waking the older woman.

"Since about ten minutes after you left." Rosie turned off the television and plunged the room into semidarkness. "I could have been doing anything. I could have walked out the door and disappeared. I could have been halfway to Oregon by now."

"I'm glad you aren't." He set the bag on the kitchen counter and pulled out the milk and cheese to put in the refrigerator. Yes, he was late. Again. And disappointed to discover that Rosie still thought about going back to her mother.

What did he expect? He was hardly ever here for her. Less than usual, lately. But what could he do about it?

This Tidewaters job was their best chance to begin a solid future together. He'd have to try harder to make everything work out.

Try harder. Work harder. God, how much more could he do?

As much as he needed to do. There was no other choice.

He returned to the front room and stopped near the sofa, sliding his hands into his pockets. "I'm glad you didn't leave," he said again. "I'm glad you're still here."

Rosie shot him a nasty glance. "She doesn't even realize you've walked in. We could have been murdered, both of us." She tossed aside the remote. "Some baby-sitter she is."

"She's all we've got."

Neva snorted and shifted, listing to one side. "Lucky us," Rosie said.

Quinn leaned down to flip the switch on the table lamp and gently placed a hand on Neva's shoulder. "Neva."

"Mmm. Umm? What?" She licked her lips and straightened. "Oh, my. You're back. Must have dozed off." She yawned hugely. "What time is it?"

"Just after ten." He extended a hand and helped her up. "Want me to walk you to your place?"

"Down the hall? Don't be silly," she said around another yawn. "I won't get lost." She waved away his thanks, but she accepted the roll of bills he pressed into her hand as he let her out the door.

"Where were you?" Rosie's tone was more hostile than ever.

"I told you. I had a meeting. And then I stopped by the site to do some paperwork."

"Yeah. Right."

Quinn shoved a hand through his hair as exhaustion settled over him like a suffocating quilt. "We'll discuss it in the morning."

"That's what you always say, and then we never do." Rosie crossed her arms over her chest. "I wasn't sure you were coming back."

"Of course I—"

The news. She must have watched Gregorio's version of the day's events on TV. And suspected her father would use a late-night business meeting as a cover while he headed out to ease his latest troubles with something alcoholic.

He closed his eyes and dug deep, mucking through the dregs of whatever had propelled him through the long day, searching for patience and enough energy to get him past this final crisis. And then he settled on the sofa beside her, in the dark, longing to reach for her hand. Craving the comfort of a simple, uncomplicated, freely given touch. It had been so long, for both of them.

She was only a child, but because she was his child, she'd had to do a lot of growing up ahead of schedule. And because she was his child, and because he wanted her in his life, it was time for him to share that life with her. All of it, the good and the bad.

The dregs, if that was all he had to offer.

"I wanted a drink today," he said, "but I dealt with it."

He waited, but she didn't respond. She sat very still, her pointy chin angled close to her chest, as if she were staring at the hands folded in her lap. Her little-girl profile was outlined in the dim light, and she looked too young and fragile to deal with what he had to tell her.

"There are still times I think that would be the easiest way to deal with the crap I have to put up with," he said.

"To take a drink—just one drink—and shut it all out. And God, I want that drink so bad sometimes I don't see how I can make it through the next minute without tasting the burn. But then I think of you, and I know you'll be here, waiting for me, and it keeps me straight."

He swallowed and struggled to get the spit down his tight throat. A different kind of burn there was making it hard to force out the words. "You're the biggest reason I have for keeping straight, Rosie. I know that's a lot of pressure to put on you, but that's how it is."

"Then you mustn't have thought I was a good enough reason before. You didn't even—"

Her voice broke, and she smashed her lips together and dashed her knuckles over her face. He noticed the glint of moisture smeared on her cheek, and he wanted more than anything to reach out and pull her into his arms and hold her until the pain disappeared. But he couldn't do that for her, not now. Right now it was more important to listen to what she had to say, even though he knew it would probably flay them both wide open.

"Say it, Rosie. You can say anything. There's nothing you can say that's any worse than what I've said to myself, a dozen times."

"You didn't try before. You didn't love me before." Her voice rose, thin and keening. "You don't love me now. Not really."

"At times like this, when I come home so late, I'm sure it must seem that way." He shook his head. "But you know—deep down inside, you know only part of that's true. Tell me you know that, Rosie. Tell me the truth."

Her chest rose and sank with jagged, silent sobs, and he couldn't stand it any longer, couldn't wait any longer. He reached for her, and the fact that she was hurting enough to let him wrap her in his arms made his throat ache so bad he thought he'd die. "Rosie, Rosie," he crooned as he stroked the back of her head and her tears soaked the front of his shirt. "I do love you. So much. More than anything. We'll figure this out, I promise."

He waited until she'd relaxed and slumped against him, exhausted by the late hour and the emotional storm. He ran his fingers through her hair and wondered if he should arrange for it to be trimmed. Maybe he could take her out to lunch this weekend, add in a little shopping and a trip to a beauty parlor. Did beauty parlors take little girls as customers?

He could ask Sylvie, he supposed, when he stopped by to check on Ned. Or Tess—he'd ask Tess. She'd love having one more opportunity to tell him what to do.

Rosie sniffed. "Are you going to send me back?"

Quinn squeezed his eyes shut, dreading the next question. But he had to ask. He owed it to Rosie. "Do you want to go?"

She didn't answer at first, and he felt as though the rest of his life hung suspended in the silence. "Sometimes," she said at last.

He blew out the breath he'd been holding. "Thank you for being honest about that." *Thank you for not saying yes.*

"Do you want to send me back sometimes?"

"Never." He straightened and drew her back so he could look her in the eye. "I want you to stay with me, Rosie. Not just for a while, while your mom's making up her mind about what to do with her life. I want you to stay with me for good."

He cleared his throat, as nervous as he'd been when

he'd asked her mother to marry him. "Will you stay with me, Rosie? I know it's been hard making this move, leaving your friends and your school. And I know it's tough being so far from your mom. But I like having you here. I've got plans—good plans—for us both."

She sniffed again and ran her hand beneath her nose. "What plans?"

"A house. I've been saving up for a house. I want you to have a big yard and a room for watching TV with your friends when they come over."

"Could we have a swimming pool?"

He smiled. "I suppose we could plan for that, too."

"Could we have a dog?"

"Didn't I mention a dog?" He pulled her into another tentative hug, elated when she didn't stiffen or resist. "I've been wanting one of those, too. For a long time."

"Remember Banjo?" She yawned. "Could we get one like Banjo?"

"Sure."

At the moment, he would have promised her anything. But it was late, and there was school tomorrow. And work. He yawned and finished it off with a tired groan, and his smart girl took the hint. "Guess it's time for bed," she said.

"Guess so."

"Dad?"

"Yeah?"

"Since I had to stay up so late tonight to wait for you, I'm probably going to be too tired to make my lunch in the morning. Can I have money for a hot lunch tomorrow?"

Smart girl, all right. He leaned to the side and pulled his wallet from his back pocket. "Is a five enough?"

"Yep." She plucked the bill from his fingers, and he knew he'd never see the change.

Women.

Rosie, Geneva, Tess, his ex. Why did all the women in his life have to be so smart—and cost him so much?

CHAPTER ELEVEN

THE ANNUAL University Foundation wine tasting was one of Geneva's least favorite social events. She rarely enjoyed the local wines, she rarely wanted to bid on the auction items and she rarely cared for the conversation. But since she was one of this year's organizers, she considered it her duty to arrive early and stay late.

She meandered through the noisy crowd in the Breakers Country Club banquet room, smiling at acquaintances and checking on details. Though it was a Thursday evening, the turnout was gratifying. The string quartet arranged by the music department was an improvement over last year's guitar-playing duo. And the wine-tasting stations had been arranged to promote circulation rather than long lines.

Geneva's good friend Maudie Keene waved to her from a table set along the far wall, where she'd been busy serving a surprisingly passable Riesling. Geneva had asked her to volunteer this evening, and Maudie had in turn asked her fiancé, Geneva's cousin Ben, to assist. Maudie was radiant tonight in her new black dress and chic hairstyle. And Ben was looking his very best looking at Maudie.

Ah, love, with its talent for adding blushes and bounces and complications to life. Geneva had asked Maudie, again, when she and Ben were going to set a date. Maudie had skimmed her fingers through her auburn waves with a laugh and told her, again, that she'd be the third to know.

Geneva smiled as she sipped her Chardonnay and moved toward the buffet. Perhaps she'd offer Maudie the Chandler House gardens for her own wedding—an incentive to set a date before summer's end. It had been far too long since Chandler House had been the scene of so many happy occasions.

"Well, Geneva, it's good to see a smile on your face, considering all the bad luck you've been having on your building project." Howard Cobb stepped into her path, gesturing with his wine and nearly sloshing it over the rim of his glass. "Or should I say, all the bad breaks?"

"Stick with 'luck,' Howard. The other phrasing isn't as clever a pun as you obviously thought it might be."

He moved uncomfortably close and turned to face the room, standing shoulder-to-shoulder with her as if they were old friends trading observations on the gathering. "Speaking of bad luck," he said, "I saw that bit on Channel Six about the latest accident at Tidewaters. Your contractor seems to have more than his fair share of it."

"Perhaps." She took another sip. "And perhaps there are more logical explanations for the damage and injuries."

Howard grunted and nodded a greeting to a passing university prof. "Explanations?"

"Pouring sand into a piece of equipment isn't a cause of bad luck. It's a criminal offense. And the police are investigating the cause of Ned's fall from the scaffolding. There are some doubts about whether that was an accident."

"They should be investigating, then." Howard leaned

closer and lowered his voice. "Although it sounds like exactly the same thing happened on another of Quinn's jobs. Maybe you should have done a little more checking into his background before you hired him."

"It's suprisingly generous of you to take such an active interest in my business affairs, Howard." Geneva signaled to one of the college-student servers and placed her empty glass on the offered tray. "And since you do, I'll share some more information. I signed another lease agreement today. For one of Tidewaters' largest office spaces."

She turned to face him. "Bradley and Garbett have decided they'd like to move their firm to a waterfront location after all."

Howard's face darkened, flushed with obvious anger. "I had an understanding with Bradley."

"And now I have a lease with them both."

"We'll see if they keep it."

Geneva kept her expression pleasant and serene as a nasty chill raced through her at the threat behind his words. "Yes, we'll see."

"Howard?" Ben joined them and clapped a hand on the councilman's shoulder. "I thought that was you. How's that son of yours enjoying college? He's in San Diego, right?"

Howard turned toward Ben as Maudie appeared with a glass of champagne. "Here," she said quietly as she handed it to Geneva. "You look like you could use this."

"I'm not sure about the bubbles at the moment, but thanks." Geneva took a tiny sip and sighed. "Thanks for coming to my rescue, but who is manning your station?"

"One of the grad students—a theater major. I told him I needed a break, and he jumped at the chance. Creep," she said, with a daggered look for Howard. "I saw him leaning in close, looking for all the world as if you and he were old chums sharing a big secret. Ugh."

"I did share a secret with him. I told him I stole one of his tenants today."

"You didn't." Maudie laughed and finger-combed her bangs.

"I did." Geneva's tension eased, and she managed a small smile. "Tess and I took Jim Bradley and Jason Garbett out to lunch, and then she gave them a tour of some of the design work in her office. Jason is thinking of hiring her to do a vacation home for him next year." Her smile widened. "My granddaughter is quite the saleswoman, if I do say so myself."

"Takes after her grandmother."

"Perhaps." Geneva lifted her flute. "I think I might be in a champagne mood after all."

THE FORECASTED STORM blew in on Thursday night, pummeling the Tidewaters site with rain and bullying whitecaps across the bay. Quinn canceled Friday's construction plans and holed up that morning in the office trailer.

Shortly before noon, a battered blue pickup pulled into the small parking area beside his truck. Quinn rose from his desk chair and rounded the counter to open the door. "Hey, Steve."

"Mornin', Quinn." Steve Wade stomped into the stuffy room and shook the wet from his slicker. He'd put on a few pounds since he'd worked on Quinn's crew. And picked up a tremor in his hands since his days as Quinn's number-one drinking buddy. "How're things?" he asked in a falsely cheerful voice.

"Can't complain." Quinn moved behind the counter,

uneasy with Steve's cadaverlike grin and the overpowering smell of mint on his breath. "Yourself?"

"Fine. Just fine. You'd never know what happened all those years ago. Medical science is a miracle, and I'm living proof. Walking proof," Wade corrected with an unpleasant chuckle. He glanced around the office and then leaned in to squint at Rosie's picture. "This Rosie?"

"Yeah."

"Growing up fast, isn't she? Sure is getting pretty. Just like her momma." Wade strolled in a casual circle around the compact space, making a show of checking things out. "Heard Rosie's back with you."

"That's right." Quinn wanted to wait him out, but he wanted him gone more. "What can I do for you, Steve?"

"Well, now, I'm not sure that's the right question." Wade quit his wandering to slouch against the counter, and Quinn noticed the sickly red rimming his eyes. Drinking again. Or using something else to get him through the day.

"The right question," Wade continued, "is what can I do for you?"

"I don't need any help on this job, if that's what you're here about."

Wade dropped the former-buddy act and gave Quinn a squinty-eyed stare. "Heard another man got hurt here this week."

"That's right."

"Just like old times."

"No." Quinn kept his voice steady and his eyes on Wade's. "It wasn't anything like what happened to you."

"Is that so?" Wade lifted one brow over a long, hard stare, giving memory time to drip its bitterness into the silence. And then his lips thinned in another smile as he dropped his gaze to his hands and rubbed a spot on one of his thumbs. "Well, I stopped by today 'cause I figured I could help you out some. Maybe take his place."

"I figured that might be the reason for this visit. But I've already got it covered."

Wade's grin faded. "Well, now. That's convenient."

"I don't think Ned would agree with that."

"Look here, Quinn." Wade curled his hand into a fist on the counter and then spread his shaking fingers wide. "You owe me."

Quinn nodded, acknowledging the sentiment, if not the fact. "I paid that debt a long time ago."

"Some debts can't never be paid in full."

"This isn't one of them."

Quinn moved around the counter and strode to the door. He opened it wide and stood, holding the knob in place while the wind flung the cold and wet in to lash at his clothes and spit on the dusty floor.

Wade's eyes roamed over Quinn's features as though he were searching for a change of heart. Or a sign of weakness. At last he straightened, tugged the slicker's hood over his head and walked out the door. "See you around, Quinn."

Quinn didn't respond. There was nothing more to say than what he'd already said a dozen times. And no way to respond to the menace coiled in Wade's parting words.

TESS LEANED a shoulder against one of her office windows facing Main Street on Friday, frowning at the whitecaps frosting the waves on the bay. Things were getting nasty out there. It was a good thing she'd slipped out to get a midafternoon double-caramel latte before the storm had gathered strength. Now moaning gusts of wind drove fat drops against the glass, and the sky was so smudged with gray she'd switched on her desk lamp to add an extra bit of light to her darkened work space.

Not that she intended to sit and produce something… productive. It was Friday afternoon, after all, and there wasn't anything on her desk that couldn't wait until Monday. Hell, there was nothing on her desk, not even dust. She'd spent the morning straightening her snack counter, filing her notes, rearranging her paper clips and pencils and wiping down her phone and keyboard. Now the remainder of the day stretched ahead, with nothing to fill it but a low-level craving for caffeine she didn't need and an invitation for a drink at the Shanty-man she didn't want.

No, she didn't want to hang out at the usual bar and stare at the usual crowd. She might not know the reason for her restlessness, but she knew it wouldn't be cured by flirting with some local guy or rehashing the local gossip. She'd call Addie and suggest an alternative—sharing a takeout dinner and kicking back with a rented movie instead of dressing for a girls' night out. Or maybe they could invite themselves to Charlie's house and give Jack a bad time.

Another slap of wind rattled the glass, and a crooked lightning dagger stabbed through the bruised clouds to the south. Tess sipped the last of her cooling drink and didn't quite count to three before the thunder rumbled along Main Street. Definitely a night to cozy up with friends instead of perching on a hard bar stool. She couldn't think of a takeout meal she'd like to eat or a movie she'd like to see at the moment, but she could coast along on Addie's choices.

Now if she could just work up the enthusiasm to cross the room and pick up the phone.

A big black truck pulled to the curb outside her shop as another boom of thunder rolled down the street like a runaway bass drum. Her pulse kicked up with annoyance, and she realized an argument with Quinn would be a more effective method of filling her afternoon and revving up her system than a second cup of caramel latte.

She opened the door, flipping the Open sign to Closed as he walked in. "Too wet to work?" she asked.

"Too windy." He pulled off his Keene Concrete gimme cap and combed his fingers through his hair. "Too stormy to draw plans?"

"Too depressing." She dropped her empty cup into the tiny metal bin near the entrance and followed him to the back of her office. "Speaking of depressing—how's Ned?"

"Healing, but grouchy as a pack of grizzlies, according to Sylvie."

"Poor thing."

"Ned? Or Sylvie?" Quinn rolled his hat and stuffed it into his jacket pocket. "Seems to me she got the worst end of the deal."

"No argument there."

He unfastened several jacket snaps. "Got a minute?"

"Got several of them as it turns out." She waved a hand at a row of decorative pewter doorknob hooks along one wall as he shrugged out of his heavy, soaked jacket. "You can hang that there."

He did as she'd asked and then turned to face her. "Sylvie told me you dropped by with a casserole dinner a couple of nights ago. Nice of you."

"Don't act so surprised, Quinn." Tess strolled toward her desk. "I can be nice when the mood hits."

"She said she had no idea what was in it. The kids were afraid to eat it at first."

"I'll bet they loved it."

He grinned. "Every bite."

She grinned back at him, and it struck her that this was the first time she'd ever seen him smile. Really, truly smile. And omigod, his was breathtaking. She hadn't imagined precisely how that tanned skin would stretch over those angular bones or how much amusement could be packed into the tiny lines fanning from the corners of his eyes.

A flash of lightning brightened the office and tickled the current to the fixtures. One. Two. A combination crack-and-boom rattled the windows.

His smile faded. "I hired someone to replace Ned," he said.

"So soon?"

Quinn's jaw tightened, and a tiny muscle jumped along the edge. He wasn't happy about arranging for a replacement, either. "Mick O'Shaughnessy," he said. "Seems like a nice enough guy. Knows a lot about general construction. Specializes in finish carpentry, so I might keep him on after Ned gets back. If he'll stay. He's a ball player."

"Ball?"

"Baseball. Arranged to get himself traded to the Wildcats for the rest of the season." Quinn frowned. "I sure hope I can work around his schedule."

"Shouldn't it be the other way around?"

"Good help is hard to find. Expert help even harder."

"Well." She leaned one hip against the edge of her desk. "I suppose you know best how to schedule your crew. Thanks for letting me know."

"That's not all I came to talk to you about."

She folded her arms across her chest. "Oh?"

"I came to talk to you about the sidewall insulation."

Right on cue, her blood pressure notched up a few points. Another tug-of-war over the specs. She knew the routine, knew what to expect, had gone this round many times before, on other jobs in other places.

She knew she shouldn't let it bother her so much, but this was Quinn pulling at the other end of the rope. And the fact that she seemed to have an over-the-top reaction to everything to do with this man only added to her irritation. "What about it?" she asked.

"Seems to me the R-factor is a little high for this area."

"It's well within state regulations."

"It's a big state," he said, "with a lot of extremes."

"I don't think it's out of line."

"It's excessive. And expensive," he said in his oh-so-reasonable voice. "It doesn't have to be either of those."

"It's in the specs list," she said, "and therefore, something you were aware of before we started this project. Part of the package you bid on—and therefore, something that's in the budget."

One corner of his mouth lifted. "I thought a woman like you could come up with a new argument instead of falling back on that tired old line about the budget."

She narrowed her eyes. "What do you mean, a woman like me?"

The other half of his mouth curved up in a sly grin. "Changing the R-factor to a local standard might save enough to pay for more of those fancy windows your friend makes, among other things."

"You didn't answer my question."

"It wasn't about the job."

She straightened from the desk and edged closer to him. Another streak of lightning flickered like a strobe across his features, and another clap of thunder exploded overhead. She forgot to start her countdown, but before her heart could beat once, a deep vibration shook the room.

"Is this part of the trouble you warned me about the other night?" she asked.

"I don't know." His gaze swept over her, over the flush she could feel spreading across her cheeks, and the nipples thrusting against the silvery silk of her blouse and the warm, liquid weight settling low in her belly beneath her black crepe skirt.

"That depends on what kind of trouble you want," he said, and his voice seemed to roll through her like the elements.

He grew unnaturally still as he stared at her, and the moments ticked by in an increasingly unbearable tension as she absorbed and reflected his scrutiny. She was beginning to understand why he did this, why he shut everything else out and took her in like this. His gaze was like foreplay—testing and teasing without the use of his hands. Awareness crackled like static over her sensitized skin, and her body pulsed with the dull throb of anticipation.

She ran her tongue over her lower lip. "Why don't you just kiss me and get it over with?"

"Why don't I?"

He wrapped his long, rough fingers around her arms and drew her close. "I'm probably going to regret this when it's over."

Her head tipped back, and her lashes drifted low. "Why wait until then to figure it out? I already know this is a big mistake."

One of his legs brushed against hers as he shifted still closer. "So why do you want to go through with it?"

"I've already warned you. I'm a terrible person." She skimmed her palms up his sides, savoring the sensation of warm, soft shirt stretched over hard, shifting muscle. "I have a lot of trouble denying myself the things I want."

"I don't." His fingers tightened, and then he eased his grip and lowered his hands to her waist. "Not usually, anyway. You seem to be the one exception to all my rules."

"Golly, Quinn. You sure know how to make a girl feel special." She gasped and shivered as he tugged the hem of her blouse from her skirt's waistband. "And you don't have to worry. I'll try to make this as easy as possible for both of us."

"I appreciate it," he said.

She raised her arms to his shoulders and tangled her fingers in his thick black hair. It was still damp from the storm and warm with the energy emanating from his body. She pressed closer, craving more of that heat for herself.

His head lowered toward hers, and his mouth was a tantalizing fraction of an inch away. "Any requests?" he asked.

"You mean, like do I want it fast and hot?"

The crinkles at the sides of his eyes deepened. "Maybe I could talk you into slow and easy."

"You could try, but neither of us has that much time to waste."

"Kissing me won't be a waste of your time."

"Prove it," she said.

CHAPTER TWELVE

QUINN'S HANDS were shaking. He tightened his grip on the slippery, satiny thing Tess wore beneath her shirt and held on as if it were a lifeline and he were sinking, sinking, struggling for breath, his heart pounding. It couldn't be true; he wasn't a young boy touching his first girlfriend for the first time. He was a grown man with enough experience to be appalled at this dry-mouthed, weak-kneed reaction to the feel of a woman's body against his and the warm, moist rush of her breath across his face.

But he wanted desperately to dazzle her, to make her desire him the way he desired her. He wanted to make her forget all the other men she'd ever kissed, ever made love with. He wanted this kiss to spin out, to go on and on, to scatter her thoughts and set her on fire. He wanted so much—too much. This one thing mattered too much.

Too late. Her lashes fluttered and drifted down over her wonderful, whiskey-hued eyes, and her lips parted on a soft sigh, and then he was closing the last charged sliver of space between them and covering her mouth with his.

Dark, rich flavors coasted over pliancy and heat—coffee and silk and sin. He brushed his lips against hers, again and again, drawing out the moment, tempting her with promises, savoring his delight, chaining his greed.

Their mouths slipped, caught, moved over each other's in moist, delicious friction as she pressed against him and he drew her still nearer, crushing her breasts against the thin wall of his chest, against his hammering heart.

Her fresh, flowery scent surrounded him, seeped inside and wound through him as his hands stroked up her sides, sliding beneath airy fabric to the layer of warm silk that was her skin. His hands fanned across her narrow back to gather her tighter, closer. Rain burst against her windows like machine-gun fire, and thunder roared into the room to shake them both. He swallowed her sigh and thrilled to the lingering vibration of her moan within his embrace.

Yes, he thought as she turned her head and bared her throat to his lips. *Yes,* he breathed as her hands clutched his hair and pulled him back to her ravening mouth. *Yes,* he groaned as her body rubbed against his. *Yes, yes.*

Past arousal, past care, he sank mindlessly into the moment and made hot, languid love to her mouth, pouring the weeks of frustration and craving into each teasing nibble, each luxurious bite, straining against her, wanting more, needing more, needing…Tess. And losing himself to her in the bargain.

She'd completely dazzled him.

The next clap of thunder broke the enslaving trance that had come over him, and he drew her away, regretting the loss of contact, grateful for the lingering taste of her on his lips. "Proof enough?" he asked in a voice hoarse with strain.

"Hmm?" She blinked once, twice, as her eyes slowly focused on his and a charming blush flooded her cheeks. "Oh. Yeah."

Her hands slid down his shirtfront to her waist to tug

on a jacket that wasn't there, and her pink cheeks reddened as she fumbled and stuffed her blouse back into her skirt. "Not bad, Quinn," she said. "Not bad at all."

Near the front of her office, a ringing buzzer interrupted their conversation. An instant later, another clock jumped and jangled on the counter behind them, its harsh metallic clanging competing with the obnoxious beeping from her computer.

"Shit," said Tess as she tugged her purse from a desk drawer. "Shit, shit, shit. No quarters. Do you have any?"

"Quarters?" Quinn reached into his pockets, uncertain whether he'd heard her correctly.

"You know—twenty-five cents," she said. "Quarters. Do you have any?"

He pulled out a fistful of change. "How many do you need?"

"All of them." She tossed her purse on her desktop and began rummaging through another drawer. "I never have enough. Damn it, I hate to use dimes. Dimes mess up my entire system."

"Here." He dropped three quarters into her outstretched palm.

"Thanks." She grabbed a big black umbrella from a slim metal bin and dashed out her door.

He followed as far as the front of the office and stood, jangling the rest of the change in his pocket and staring out the Main Street window while she battled the wind for control of her umbrella. She reached the curb near her red roadster and huddled over a meter, her hair whipping around her face and her shirttail flapping against her rain-spattered butt as she slid coins through the tiny meter slots.

A guy had to respect a woman who could stick to her principles even when it wasn't convenient.

As she rushed back to the office, one of her open-toed shoes splashed through a puddle, and she danced to the side, her mouth moving in what he imagined was some pretty inventive cursing. The muttering continued when her umbrella caught in the bell above her entry.

"Let me help you with that," he said, reaching toward the metal strap on the transom window.

"No need. I've got it." She yanked the umbrella free, slammed the door behind her and leaned against it, her breasts rising and falling beneath her dampened shirt. "I'll pay you back."

"That's okay." He carefully removed any trace of amusement from his features. "The show was worth the price of admission."

She wrestled with the umbrella strap and then simply shoved the sodden mess back into the bin and plopped into her desk chair. "Look. About what just happened—"

"I understand. It's the principle of the thing."

She looked adorably confused for a second, and then she frowned. "I don't want to talk about it."

"About the meter?"

Her eyes narrowed. "Not. One. word."

"What do you want to talk about?"

"The kiss. Kissing. You and me…kissing." She toed off her wet shoes and rubbed one foot over the other. "This isn't going to cause problems for us on the site, is it?"

"Not unless you go looking for trouble."

"Is that what this is?" she asked, her mouth curving with a seductive smile. "Trouble?"

He moved behind her desk, turned her chair to face him, placed his hands on its arms and leaned over her.

"Lady, you've been trouble since the moment I first laid eyes on you."

She ran one of her feet over the top of his boot. "I like the sound of that."

"Figured you would."

Her smile faded. "I don't set out to cause trouble, you know."

"I wouldn't be working with you if I thought you did."

He allowed himself the pleasure of looking at her. Of noticing the way her lashes spiked and her hair waved when it was wet, the way her perfume rose from her skin as it warmed, the way her shirt lay open along the curve of her throat and draped along the slope of her breast. The way her toes splayed over the laces of his boots. He steeled himself for the torture of taking in just this, and nothing more, and when the pain grew exquisite, when he knew he was about to lean in and press his lips to hers again, he straightened and allowed himself one more thing. He slowly trailed one finger along the back of her long, slender hand, enjoying the textures of warm skin, ridged knuckle and slick polish before breaking the contact.

He retrieved his jacket from the hook on the wall and shrugged into it as he crossed the office toward her door. Without a backward glance, he pulled on his cap, flipped up his collar and stepped into the storm. The cold, stinging rain hammered some sense back into him, and he realized they'd never settled the business that had brought him to her office.

Idiot. Liar, he added as he climbed into his truck. Business hadn't brought him here—he could have discussed the specs with her over the phone. But he couldn't have watched confusion cloud her eyes or breathed in her floral scent from the phone in his dreary trailer. He couldn't have teased her or tempted himself with the possibility of a kiss, and he couldn't have sampled the sweet coffee taste of her or run his hands over her amazing skin.

He couldn't have faced the long holiday weekend without being near her once more, just for a few minutes.

With his truck idling at the curb outside her office, he fumbled in his deep, damp jacket pocket for his cell phone and punched in her number. "Tess."

"You again."

"Yeah."

"Change your mind about the specs?"

"Is that why you kissed me?"

"You know, we could discuss kissing over the phone, if you'd like. Or you could come back inside, and we could pick up our discussion right where we left off."

"Or we could discuss it this weekend."

Her slight pause had him writhing inside, just the way he used to suffer when he was seventeen and begging girls for dates.

"That works for me," she said at last.

"How about my place?" He cringed when he realized what he'd done, but withdrawing the invitation seemed worse than carrying through with this half-brained idea. "Dinner, tomorrow night."

"I'll bring the food. You bring a change of mind about those specs."

He gave her his address, agreed to a meeting time and disconnected. And then he stared through the streaks of water on his window, straining for another glimpse of her.

Foolish. Worse than foolish, he thought as he pulled

from the curb and considered the logical outcome of a dinner date with Tess at his apartment.

Rosie would kill them both.

TESS SKIRTED the large stain on the third-floor hallway as she made her way toward Quinn's apartment the following afternoon. The Barlow Building's exterior was charmingly vintage; the interior was heavy on the vintage and light on the charm. Still, what looked like the original lighting fixtures hung from lofty ceilings, and the shoulder-high paneled wainscotting was fabulous. The doorways she passed wore elaborate trim and fanciful transom crowns of tinted, pebbled glass. Definitely some possibilities here, if someone would invest in basics such as paint and plaster. Some new flooring wouldn't hurt, either, she thought as her sandal heel snagged in a threadbare section of carpet.

A solid foundation and attractive structural elements hidden beneath layers of neglect and indifference. Much like the man who lived here. He cleaned up well, she'd discovered that night at Charlie's house. His sense of humor might be low-key, but she was beginning to appreciate the subtlety. And his kisses—oh, yeah, there were lots of possibilities there.

Thinking about those possibilities had her stomach fluttering and her pulse skipping as she approached the end of the hall. She couldn't remember now what it was she'd been expecting from Quinn, but it hadn't come close to what he'd done to her in a few moments and a few touches. He'd had her breathless, he'd had her boneless, and in a short while he'd have had her begging him to drag her down onto her office floor and…

She stopped and gave her floaty kimono-style top a neatening tug. And then she juggled her briefcase, a sack of groceries and a Bern's Bakery box onto one arm, lifted her free hand and knocked on the door of apartment number 305. A few moments later, a gangly girl with Quinn's dark hair and solemn eyes opened the door.

"Hi, there. You must be Rosie." Tess shifted her load while waiting for a response, but Quinn's daughter had obviously inherited her father's annoying habit of silent, motionless staring.

"Rosie." Quinn's voice growled from somewhere deep inside the apartment. "Let her in."

The kid turned and disappeared, leaving Tess to catch the door with her foot before it closed in her face. Tempted to retreat, she sucked in a deep breath, bared her teeth in a delightfully social smile and elbowed her way into the war zone.

Rosie had curled in a defensive pose on an ugly brown sofa, the television remote clutched in one fist. Tess recognized the hostile slouch; she'd spent much of her own childhood in the same position. "Always a good plan to be nice to the lady with the food, kid," she said.

"We've already got food. And I'm not a kid." Rosie aimed the remote at the television. Rock music blared through the room.

Tess found it easy to ignore the change in volume, since she'd been momentarily stunned by the decor. It was like being buried alive, surrounded by unrelenting earth tones, smothered by the scents of dust and decay. She caught a glimpse of peeling olive-green paper in what she guessed was a bathroom and shuddered.

The noise crept up another level. "When you're standing on this side of thirty," Tess said, raising her voice over the mayhem on the screen, "anyone younger looks like a kid."

"Maybe you need glasses."

And maybe you need an attitude adjustment.

Quinn entered the room, confiscated the remote and switched off the TV. "Hi," he said as he pocketed Rosie's weapon. "Let me take some of that."

"Thanks." Tess passed him the grocery bag. She lowered her briefcase to the floor near the table and followed him into a kitchen that had seen better days—and all of them in the fifties. At least the brown had disappeared. Too bad it had been replaced by aqua and pink.

"I kept it simple," she said. "Tri-tips, salad, baguettes. And for dessert, a cream cake from Bern's."

"Sounds great." He set the bag on the flamingo-colored counter, pulled out a plastic packet filled with the marinating steaks and then stepped back, wiping his hands on his jeans. "I—I don't have much in the way of cooking tools."

Flustered was a new and interesting look on him. A very appealing look. Enjoying his discomfort far more than she should, she crossed her arms and slouched with a shoulder against one wall. "Why am I not surprised?"

"I don't eat red meat." Rosie stood guard in the wide doorway. "And I don't like salad."

Quinn frowned. "You love salad. And since when don't you eat red meat?"

"Since I learned about the harmful effects of cattle on the environment. Not to mention how fattening beef can be," the kid added with an innocent glance at Tess. "I've heard it can give you cellulite. Some people need to worry about that more than others."

Tess gave her a wide smile. "Good thing I'm not one of them. I have an amazing metabolism. Not to mention an endless supply of patience."

"You're going to need it," Quinn muttered as his daughter sauntered back to the front room. "Sorry about that."

"No need to apologize. I expected a reaction of that sort." Which was why she shouldn't let the kid get to her, Tess reminded herself as she pulled her salad ingredients from the bag. Not her daughter, not her problem. Thank God. "I'm a potentially threatening female trespassing on her territory."

"Could the fight for female dominance be fatal to the men in the immediate vicinity?"

"Only if they don't do the dishes." She opened a cabinet, searching for a large bowl and a shallow baking dish. "If I were you, I'd be more worried about the crap they're teaching kids in school these days."

She paused in her hunt and glanced over her shoulder at Quinn. He was studying her with his usual stony intensity, but she thought she detected a trace of something different—something softer—in his features tonight. Something twining around her heart and trapping too much inside.

"What's wrong?" she asked him, because she didn't want to have to answer that question herself.

"I thought it would be strange to see you here. In my place." He pulled the remote from his pocket and set it on the counter before taking one hesitant step closer. "To be with you here, like this."

"You did?" Heart pounding, she busied herself by turning the oven on. "Is it strange?"

He shook his head.

She carefully arranged the meat in the baking dish she'd found, excruciatingly aware of his every move, inexplicably nervous with the warmth of his gaze and the turn the conversation had taken. "If you thought this would be so strange, why did you invite me?"

"I don't know."

Beyond the front room, a door slammed.

"Wrong answer," Tess said.

Wrong situation. Wrong idea, coming here. Wrong man, for her. Wrong, wrong, wrong.

But still, she wanted him. With every shaky breath she dragged in past ribs that squeezed so tightly she was sure her lungs would bruise.

Her social smile stiffened at the corners, taking on a determined edge. "You're going to have to come up with a better reason before dessert."

CHAPTER THIRTEEN

AN HOUR LATER, Quinn stared at the delicious but half-eaten food on his plate. He felt as though he were a bone being tugged and gnawed at both ends by a couple of nasty-tempered terriers. Rosie had been surprisingly talkative throughout the meal, politely asking Tess all sorts of embarrassing questions. And Tess hadn't batted an eye as she provided equally embarrassing answers.

"That's enough," he said after Rosie's latest poke at their guest. "Tess and I have work to do, and you have homework to finish up."

"Already done." Rosie set her napkin by her plate and stood. "I'll do the dishes."

"Thank you," said Tess. She lifted her plate, but Rosie ignored it, passing her by to take Quinn's things from the table before heading to the kitchen.

"Don't say it," Tess said before he could apologize again.

He stewed in another awkward silence as Rosie returned to collect the serving pieces and made another trip to the kitchen, leaving Tess's place setting behind.

Tess nonchalantly stacked her things and shoved them to one end of the table. "Is it okay if we work right here?"

"This is the best spot." He brushed a few bread crumbs aside while she reached for her briefcase.

Rosie strolled through the room and sprawled on the sofa. A moment later, the television screen exploded with color and noise. Damn. He'd forgotten about the remote.

He glared at his daughter. "I thought you were doing the dishes."

"I'm letting them soak."

"Turn down the volume. Please," he added in a tone one inch shy of a snarl.

Tess rose from her seat and carried her water glass to the kitchen.

"Maybe I should go to my room." Rosie switched off the TV and stood, sparing him a wounded look as she straightened the cushions. "I wouldn't want to disturb you."

"Maybe Rosie could sit and read while we work." Tess flashed one of her dangerously sweet smiles in Rosie's direction as she carried the bakery box and a short stack of dessert plates out to the table. "Reading is so important to a child's development."

She opened the box and reached for a knife. "And I'm sure Rosie doesn't get to spend much time with you, Quinn, considering the long hours you work. Besides, I'd hate to think I'd had a part in driving her from her own front room." She paused and gave his daughter a terrifyingly brilliant smile. "And I'd really enjoy her company."

Rosie stared at the cake. And then she leveled a slitty-eyed look at Tess.

Quinn's gut twisted up so tight he feared his dinner might get stuck in some knot and sit there, festering, for the few remaining days of his life. He knew how to wedge himself, without getting clobbered, between two men facing off for a fistfight. He had no clue how to break up this female war of wills raging through his apartment without destroying them all in the process.

"Reading sounds like a good idea," he lied. He offered his daughter a weak smile. "Grab one of your books and join us. I'll build a fire."

It was summer, for crying out loud, and he had no idea if he had any kindling or if a blocked flue might fill the room with smoke. On the other hand, asphyxiation might be preferable to the dessert course.

"Sounds cozy," Tess said.

"I'll be right back." Rosie shot him her death stare, marched from the room and slammed her door.

He winced. "Do you think she'll come out and have some cake?"

"Not a chance. I wouldn't." Tess gathered the rest of her dinner things and took them to the kitchen.

She didn't come back.

A few seconds later, the kitchen plumbing wheezed and sputtered, and the sounds of dishwashing filled the kitchen. He stole a moment to shut his eyes and wallow in self-pity, wincing again when a cupboard door banged shut.

What a disaster. He should have figured Rosie would resent him bringing a woman—any woman—into their lives. Hadn't her mother dumped her on his doorstep because she had a new man in her life? If Quinn were to get involved with another woman, where would Rosie end up? Who would want her?

God. His daughter probably felt like the booby prize in the life of every adult who was supposed to care for her.

He leaned forward, his elbows on the table and his head in his hands. He had no idea how to give Rosie the reassurance she needed. He'd had plenty growing up—

his parents had loved and supported him in a simple, settled life. Even now, though they'd retired to Arizona and he seldom saw them, they'd stayed in touch. He knew he could count on them.

But his daughter had learned the hard way that she couldn't count on him.

Weighed down with guilt and regret, he hauled himself out of his chair and trudged to the kitchen doorway. Tess was wiping down the counters, her lips set in a thin, grim line. She'd stuck her short, jagged hair behind her ears, but her bangs were slipping loose, one soft strand at a time, to sway with each jerky movement. A pretty smudge of pink highlighted her curved cheekbone.

Even in a temper, she was gorgeous. Tantalizing. After all that had happened this evening, with all the obstacles that lay between them, he itched to take her into his arms and—

No. Not tonight. Not in Rosie's home.

He leaned a shoulder against the jam. "Were you like this when you were this age?"

"Worse."

"How did your parents survive?"

She dropped the sponge in the sink and twisted the tap. "They chose not to deal with me. Or with my brother. They passed us off to the servants."

"I'm sorry."

"Don't be. I was better off with the servants." She squirted soap into her hands and scrubbed furiously. "My father had his work. My mother drank."

"Then I'm twice as sorry." He stepped into the room to hand her a towel.

She dried her hands, carefully folded the towel and draped it across the edge of the sink, avoiding his gaze.

"I don't like pity," she said at last. "I don't want it, especially from you."

"Tess." He simply surrendered to the longing, drawing her close and then rationalizing the move after he'd made it, telling himself he could offer her some bit of comfort in his embrace. And if he happened to find his own comfort—and a world of pleasure—in the contact, it was a bonus that had sprung from pure and honorable intentions. "I didn't think you'd take my pity or my apology if I offered it," he said. "So I won't make that mistake."

"Again."

He grinned and lifted a hand to cup her chin. "Lady, you are one tough customer."

Her answering smile looked a little wobbly around the edges. "And don't you forget it," she whispered.

She pulled away and moved into the front room, where she placed her things back in her briefcase and zipped it shut. "I think it's time for me to go."

"We have work to do."

"It can wait." She clenched her fingers on the top of her case and then smoothed them over its edge. "The truth is, I'm ashamed of my behavior tonight. I've got twenty years on your daughter, and I used every one of them against her. I didn't fight fair."

"She started it."

"A handy excuse. But a mighty sorry one." Her eyes, when she lifted them to meet his, were shadowed. "I'm not usually this awful, Quinn. But I can be, at times."

"I'm nothing to brag about, either."

"I know. Your reputation precedes you."

He shook his head. "What a sorry pair we make."

"We have no business making a pair at all."

He panicked and scrambled for an answer, but then a depressing calm settled over him as he realized she was right. Hadn't he just been thinking the same thing? He had no business getting involved with this woman. No matter how much he wanted her.

And like everything else in his life he couldn't have—booze, tobacco, peace of mind—as soon as he'd decided to let go, the craving increased painfully. Tess understood his daughter in a way he never would. She understood him, too, in some mysterious way that allowed her to look past his faults and accept what was left. The fact that she was willing to walk away from something they both hungered for, for the sake of his daughter, made her more desirable than ever, for reasons he'd find impossible to resist.

Impossible. Hopeless. "I'll see you out," he said.

He opened the door for her and walked beside her down the hallway. "Thank you for dinner," he said. "It was good."

"Of course. I'm a terrific cook." She tossed her head in that way of hers to make her bangs fly and settle back where they belonged. Everything under control again.

"You didn't get any cake," he pointed out.

"I don't need the calories. I lied about my metabolism." She paused at the top of the stairs. "I told you— I'm a terrible person."

"I already knew that. Your reputation precedes you."

Her lips turned up at the corners, and then she leaned in and pressed a quick, casual kiss to his cheek. "Hang in there, Quinn. Your daughter cares enough about you to put up a pretty tough fight. She wouldn't have been giving me such a hard time if she didn't want to keep you all to herself. She doesn't want that part of her life to change."

"Maybe that's because she's had too much change lately."

"And maybe it's because she likes things just the way they are." Tess tilted her head to the side and gave him one of her witchy smiles. "Smart girl."

She walked down the steps to the first landing and then turned to give him a flirty, friendly goodbye wave. He lifted a hand in response, but she'd already disappeared around the corner.

He stood where he was, staring at the empty landing until he heard the muffled whump of the street-level door closing behind her. Nothing had changed since dinner. He was still trapped in the middle and pretty much chewed out.

TESS KEPT BUSY on Sunday planting annuals in her front yard and berating herself for her behavior at Quinn's, including her cowardly retreat. She spent most of the holiday Monday washing windows and reminding herself it had never been the smartest move to consider getting involved with Tidewaters' contractor on a personal basis.

By Tuesday, she was congratulating herself on a narrow escape from a sticky involvement with a recovering alcoholic and his troubled preteen daughter. Tess knew herself well enough to admit she didn't want to change her lifestyle or sacrifice her pleasures to suit the needs of an instant family. When she got married—and she was in no hurry to make that commitment—it would be to a man who'd continue to spoil her in the manner to which she'd accustomed herself.

By Wednesday, she was missing Quinn. Missing his tall, rangy form, and his long, intense stare, and his reluctant half smiles and his scorching kisses. She rubbed her arms as she stared out her Main Street office window, wishing she could rub away the lingering tingles and the unease that trailed closely behind the memories.

She had the perfect excuse to go to him—she had Tidewaters to supervise. And he had the perfect excuse to come to her—he had those specs to discuss. But those kisses and that dinner stood like twin barriers between them.

"Idiot." She stalked to the rear of her office, swept her lime-green linen jacket from one of the pewter knobs and pulled it over her lemon-print sundress. She flipped over her sign and locked her door, sighing over the quarters she'd wasted a half an hour ago on that gluttonous meter, and stepped into her car to head to the construction site. She had a job to do.

She passed her usual drive-through coffee place, since she already had enough jitters. And she nearly pulled into Bern's for a snack to ease her way with the crew, but decided Quinn might see that as a sign of weakness. "Stupid," she muttered. "I'm the one who's making the first move here."

And wasn't it monumentally stupid, she thought as she pulled through the gate at Tidewaters a few minutes later, that she was thinking in relationship phrases instead of business terms? "Snap out of it," she ordered herself.

Easier said than done, she thought a second later when she got a good look at the gorgeous shell of the building they were creating together. He'd made a start on the third floor, and the added height made the bays and angles soar. She noted the spots where corner towers would overlook the bay, where gracefully curved corbels would accent the eaves. Where tall glass doors would open to a stunning balcony.

Beautiful. And now that the boxy basics were behind them, each addition would layer on finishing touches like icing on a fanciful cake: clever rooflines, sparkling windows, inviting porches, decorative trim boards.

It might be her design, but Quinn was bringing it to life with relatively few grumbles and no flaws in the execution. Great team, great building.

She parked beside his big black truck and started toward the trailer door. It swung open, and Rusty jogged down the short metal steps, followed by a tall, good-looking man with sun-streaked hair and impressive biceps.

"Hey, pretty lady." Rusty stopped and made a show of eyeing her tote. "Bring anything good with you today?"

"No. Sorry."

"No need to apologize." Rusty snapped his gum. "I'm headed out early. Just didn't want to miss out on one of your treats."

"Aren't you going to introduce me to the pretty lady?" asked the stranger. His deep voice carried a trace of Texas.

"You mean you haven't met Tess yet?" Rusty waved a hand in her direction. "Mick O'Shaughnessy, Tess Roussel."

"The architect." Mick extended his hand. His grip was a pleasant combination of firm and gentle. His smile was a lethal blend of masculine ease and charm.

"The ball player." She wondered if he was single and how quickly she could drag Addie to the site without making the matchmaking obvious.

"Quinn's up on the northwest corner," Rusty said, "in case you're looking for him."

"I am. Thanks." Tess returned Rusty's wave as he headed for his pickup.

"I like your design." Mick studied her, his manner as casual as a stroll on the beach. "It works."

"High praise, coming from a carpenter." She brushed her bangs from her eyes. "Quinn tells me you're pretty good with finish work."

"I'm better in left field."

"That means you're a batter, too, right?"

"Cleanup."

"My, my."

Mick's smile widened. "You're just what I expected."

"And what's that?"

"Easy on the eyes and hard to get."

Tess tilted her head to the side. "Are you trying to 'get' me, Mick?"

"No way. I want to keep this job. Mostly 'cause I happen to like the boss." He leaned toward her and lowered his voice. "He's watching us right now."

She didn't need to check. Once Mick mentioned it, she could feel Quinn's gaze on her as if it were a sunlamp. Still, she lifted a hand to shield her eyes from the afternoon's glare, looked toward the partially-clad skeleton of the top level and spied Quinn's motionless form, a dark shadow against pale plywood. An uncomfortable blend of lust and longing welled up inside her, complicated by Mick's assumptions. If a newcomer had paired her with Quinn, everyone else in the Cove must have figured the relationship was a done deal.

"Jack Maguire tells me you've got a good friend who's just as easy on the eyes," Mick said.

Tess managed to work up an encouraging smile. "That would be Addie."

"Sweet name."

"Sweet woman."

"So I've heard. Maybe one of you could bring her around the ballpark some time."

"Better ask Jack," she said. "He's Mr. Little League these days."

Mick's laugh was charming, too. "Yeah, he mentioned something about that." He pulled a set of keys from a jeans pocket. "Better get going—don't want to be late to practice. See you around, Tess."

She trudged toward the north end and entered the building. Shafts of afternoon light stretched across the concrete, and the odors of freshly sawn lumber and oily solvents competed with the bay's brine. Comforting, settling odors. She breathed them in deeply and prepared to deal with Quinn. "Hello," she called.

"Up here."

Careful to avoid slivers or catch her sandals on the raw edge of one of the subtreads, she climbed the open stairway. The view was fantastic at the second level; it was even better on top. A sparkling bay, a quaint town and two strong men in T-shirts, jeans and tool belts. "Hi, there."

"Hi, Tess." Phil cocked up the toe of one boot to brace a two-by-four against his ankle and settled his circular saw over the edge. "Bring anything to eat?"

"She's not the snack wagon." Bent at the waist, Quinn pulled his tape measure from his belt and hooked it over another two-by-four.

Behind Quinn's back, Phil gave her an apologetic shrug.

She waited until she could be heard over the shriek of the saw. "Where is everyone?"

"Mick has practice," Phil told her. "Rusty left early for a dental appointment and Tom's still out of town.

His family had a reunion over the holiday weekend. We've been—"

"Three, six and three-eighths," Quinn said, cutting short the conversation. Phil dutifully picked up another piece of lumber and measured for the cut.

Tess examined the rough plumbing stubbed up through the subfloor while the men worked together to lay out and nail in the studs and header for a window in a short section of wall. "Guess you're a little short on help today," she said when the hammering had stopped.

"Is that why you're here?" Quinn lifted one end of the wall with a grunt. "To help out?"

She glanced at her canvas espadrilles and form-fitting clothes. "I'm not exactly dressed for the job."

Muscles bulging, he gave her one of his shuttered glances.

"Okay, so I forgot my hard hat, too. Bite me."

"Not while I'm on the job," he said.

On the other end of the wall section, Phil made a quiet choking sound as he helped Quinn walk the studs upright.

Tess folded her arms across her chest, ridiculously pleased with Quinn's teasing but embarrassed that she'd set herself up for it. "We never discussed those specs."

"You said they could wait."

"I didn't mean indefinitely."

"I was the one who wanted to discuss them, not you." Quinn helped Phil heft the wall into place.

She shrugged and turned to go. "Some other time, then."

"What time is it?" Quinn asked.

"Five after three," she said.

"Shit." He strained to hold the wall steady while Phil reached for a piece of bracing.

"What?" Tess stepped forward gingerly and grabbed two of the studs. "It's not going to fall, is it?"

"It's not the wall," Quinn said. "It's Rosie. I was supposed to pick her up from school five minutes ago."

"Doesn't she take the bus?"

"Long story. Damn," he said as he shifted his grip and then lifted a shoulder to blot a streak of sweat from the side of his face. "It'll be at least fifteen minutes before we get this thing secured and braced."

"I'll go get her," Tess said.

The look Quinn shot at her made her wonder if she appeared as dismayed by her offer as she felt. "I can't let you," he said.

"I can handle it, just this once." She backed away and brushed her hands over her dress. "I'm a big girl, Quinn."

"Yeah. I noticed."

She gave him a sly smile. "You're going to owe me, big-time."

"Not the R-factor." He grimaced as the wall shifted. "Anything but that."

"Anything?"

"Damn." Another bead of sweat snaked down Quinn's temple as Phil worked to set a brace. "I'm not in the best position to bargain, am I?"

"No." She stepped in close to torture him with a preview of the debt he'd owe and blew in his ear. "But I can only think of one other position I'd rather see you in."

"God." He squeezed his eyes shut and then opened one to leer at her. "Only one?"

"Well..."

"Tess," he said. "Rosie. Please."

"All right." She straightened and gave her head a

shake to jostle the bangs from her eyes. "Don't worry, Quinn. I'll bring her back. Scout's honor."

She clambered down the stairs, moving quickly to her car. Above her, Quinn bellowed for Phil to hurry the hell up. He yelled a few other things, too, when Tess turned to wave and blew him a farewell kiss.

CHAPTER FOURTEEN

TESS FLINCHED at the shrill whistle of a sash-wearing traffic director and swerved to follow a series of fat white arrows painted on the Adams Elementary School parking lot pavement. Several yards ahead of her, a row of silver and pastel SUVs and minivans inched along one by one into a wide parking area like a herd of placid cows plodding into a milking barn.

To her right—and much closer to the school buildings—beneath a spreading, leafy maple, several empty parking spaces angled toward a curb marked green for visitors and loading. And there sat Rosie Quinn, leaning against the tree's trunk, cross-legged and frown-faced.

Ignoring the frantic waves of a busty, tanned blonde wearing one of the hideous sashes, Tess cranked her steering wheel to glide into one of the handy shady spots and switched off her ignition. Blondie approached her car and halted near the front fender, arms akimbo, glaring at Tess through the windshield.

"What?" Tess muttered. "Does my car clash with the family-themed decor?"

She climbed out and nodded at Blondie with an aggressively pert smile. "How's it going?"

"Can I help you?"

Tess gave Blondie's sleeveless striped tank, tight

white shorts, bony knees and questionable flip-flops a slow once-over. "I doubt it."

"Visitors have to check in at the office," Blondie said.

"I'm not visiting."

"Are you here to pick someone up?"

"Yeah." Tess pointed at Rosie, who'd stood and lifted her backpack when Tess had exited her car. "Her."

"Then you'll have to move your car to the pick-up area," Blondie said.

"That won't be necessary." Tess crooked a come-here finger at Rosie, who continued to stand and stare at her. Damn that family trait. "I'll be gone in a minute."

Blondie crossed her arms and thrust her D-cups in Tess's direction. "Do you have permission to take this child from the premises?"

"Yeah. I do."

Rosie slid her pack from her shoulder and let it drop to the ground beside the car. "Why isn't my dad here?"

"He got held up," Tess said.

"Why did he send you?" Rosie's frown was hostile and suspicious.

"Because I said I'd come and get you."

Two taller girls had wandered toward the base of the tree, watching the scene. "Who's she?" the one wearing braces asked.

"Nobody," said Rosie.

"You can't take this child off campus unless you've signed in at the office," Blondie said.

Tess shifted to face the woman with the bad-sash attitude. "Listen. I don't know who you are. I don't even know who you think you are. But I know who this kid's dad is, and he asked me to come and pick her up. So that's what I'm doing. Picking her up."

"I'm not going," Rosie said.

Tess stalked to the passenger side and opened the door. "Get in the car."

Another Stepford traffic cop had joined Blondie. "What's going on here?"

"Stay here," Blondie said. "I'm going to report this to the office."

Rosie gave Tess a sharklike smile of her own.

"Big mistake." Tess picked up Rosie's pack and slung it onto the passenger seat. "You don't want to play this kind of game with me, kid."

"Are you threatening that child?" Stepford asked. A small crowd of kids had gathered around Rosie. Two women stood nearby, arms crossed, heads tilted toward each other, whispering while they watched.

"No," Tess said. "I'm taking her to her father. He's the threatening adult in this situation."

"That's what you think." Blondie pulled a cell phone from her pocket. "I'm calling for backup."

"Bimbo wimp," Tess muttered.

"I heard that," Stepford said. "That was extremely rude. What kind of an example is that to set for these children?"

The children in question grinned at Tess. A plump boy in camo and navy gave a thumbs-up.

"How the hell should I know?" Tess asked. "These aren't my kids."

A beefy man in a gray janitor's shirt hiked down the walk and stopped behind Blondie. "What's going on here?"

Stepford pointed at Tess. "This woman is creating a disturbance."

"The only thing disturbing around here," Tess said, "are those sashes. Butt-ugly, if you ask me."

A few snickers and some high fives from the peanut gallery put a hint of a smile on Rosie's face.

"No one's asking you anything," Blondie said, sounding a little shaky. "Except to cooperate."

"Same goes." Tess shot Rosie a narrow-eyed look and jerked her head toward her car. "Get in."

"Is she here to pick you up?" one of the tall girls asked Rosie.

"Yeah." Rosie appeared slightly less antagonistic, but she still hadn't budged from her spot.

"Cool car," one of the boys said. "How fast does it go?"

"I got it up to one-ten once near Vegas," Tess replied. "But I have a fear of death caused by skidding out of control, flipping airborne, plowing into the pavement and having the skin peeled from my body by asphalt. I'm sure someone else could do better."

"*Awesome,*" another boy said.

"Do something," Stepford told the man in the gray shirt.

He stepped from behind Blondie. "I'm going to have to ask you to come with me, ma'am."

"Bet you hate having to do it, too." Tess pulled her keys from her jacket pocket and locked her car doors. "Bet a big, strong man like you is all embarrassed about getting sucked into these ladies' scheme for domination of the parking-lot empire."

He coughed into his hand in a belated effort to disguise his grin and then jerked his head in the direction of the school building. "Are you coming quietly, or do I have to tie your hands behind your back with a plastic garbage fastener?"

"*All right,*" said one of the boys beneath the tree. "Tie her up."

"No need," Tess said. "I'll come quietly. Rosie?"

Quinn's daughter rolled her eyes but moved to stand beside Tess. "I'd better come, too. Dad wouldn't want me to sit out here, unsupervised, all afternoon on account of you got sent to the principal's office."

AN HOUR LATER, Tess held the passenger-side door of her roadster open for Rosie. "Get in, kid."

"Jeez," Rosie said as she slid into the seat. "You're such a—"

Tess slammed the door shut so she wouldn't have to listen to the rest of the rant and stalked to the driver's side. The afternoon had been a huge success, as far as she was concerned. She'd touched off a small but vocal rebellion in the office against the traffic brigade. She'd scored a fawning shoe compliment from the school secretary—a woman with fabulous taste, even if she hadn't used it for her personal enhancement. And she'd escaped from the principal's office without suspension.

"I could have kicked her liposuctioned ass," Tess said after the first silent mile.

The kid pressed her lips together and stared out the window. "Whose ass?" she asked a couple of blocks later.

"Blondie's."

"That's Mrs. Stanton." Rosie looked worried. "She's Missy Stanton's mom."

"Poor Missy."

The kid's lips twitched in a younger version of her father's almost-but-not-quite-there smile. The Quinns probably rationed their amusement to make sure it would last into the next century.

"Is Missy as stuck-up as her mom?" Tess asked.

"Worse."

"Gag." Tess turned down a side street. "Is she in your class?"

"No. She's in the fifth grade."

"What grade are you in?"

"Why do you care?"

"I don't, believe me," Tess said. "Just making conversation. It's something people do every once in a while. Your dad should give it a try."

"Where are we going?" Rosie asked as Tess made another turn.

"To get some drive-through coffee."

"You just had some coffee. At the school."

"What—are you my mother?"

"Caffeine is addictive."

"No kidding. Must be why I drink so much of it."

Rosie slumped in her seat and resumed glaring through the glass, and Tess remembered, too late, how much this girl must resent adults with addictions. "I should probably quit," she said. "Or switch to decaf."

A skinny-shouldered shrug was the only response.

"Your dad was worried about you. That's why he called while I was in the principal's office. Omigod." Tess groaned. "*While I was in the principal's office.* It sounds like I'm twelve."

The kid muttered something uncomplimentary under her breath.

"Look," Tess said, "I don't care about what happened to me. Or to you, for that matter. I was looking forward to a fight, 'cause I'm in that kind of a mood today. Okay, I'm in that kind of a mood most of the time," she admitted, "but your dad is having a rough day, and we made it a little rougher."

"He'll get over it," Rosie said with another shrug.

"So kind of you to care."

"Whatever."

"I can kick your skinny ass, too," Tess warned.

"You're not supposed to talk to me like that."

"Really?" Tess maneuvered into the short line at Java Jive. "According to whose rules?"

"My dad's."

"You treat him like dirt and then expect him to fight your battles for you—is that how it works?"

"You don't know anything about it."

"I know more than you think." Tess pulled even with the menu board. "Chocolate or vanilla shake?"

Rosie gave her a confused stare.

"What'll it be, kid?"

"Vanilla."

"Excellent choice."

Tess gave her order and then inched ahead, next in line. "My mom is an alcoholic," she said matter-of-factly. "She's been in and out of rehab so many times I've lost count. On the good days, when I was still at home, she'd stay sober long enough to pick me up from school. On the bad days, she'd forget about me, and one of my teachers would call a cab and the maid would come out and take care of the fare when I got home. Most of the time, she'd pass out right before dinner, so I'd ask my brother to help me with my homework."

Tess paid for their beverages and handed Rosie's shake to her. "My dad drank, too," she continued, "but not as much. I only found him passed out a couple of times, and then he made me feel worse when he tried to apologize. He died when I was ten years old. Drove off the side of the road and ran into a tree. For years, I thought he'd done it on purpose because of something I'd said."

She glanced toward her passenger. "Ready to break out the violin yet?"

Rosie flicked a bland glance in her direction and then focused on sucking mush up her straw.

"Your dad made you miserable for a time," Tess said, "and you probably felt guilty for hating him. You still feel that way sometimes, so you punish him for it. But punishing him just hurts you, too."

"You don't know—"

"Yeah, yeah, I know," Tess said. "I don't know anything about it."

What she did know was that she should have kept her mouth shut. The last thing a kid like Rosie Quinn needed was one more adult giving her grief. Or pity. A delicate balance, one requiring more finesse than Tess cared to bother with.

Mémère had always struck that balance with Tess, during those long summers she'd taken her in and given her a place to find some peace. Geneva may have been unable to prevent her husband's and daughter's mistakes, but she'd never wavered in her love and support for her family. And if that love sometimes seemed overly stern and the support diamond-hard, well, maybe that was what it took to keep the Chandlers' foundation from cracking.

Rosie Quinn could probably handle the tough stuff, too. Tess had a sneaking suspicion that beneath the hands-off attitude and slightly grungy exterior the kid was okay. Rosie'd probably clean up well at some point down the road, just like her dad.

They drove in silence for the remainder of the short trip and made the final turn around the corner of Quinn's block. At a third-floor window, framed by the drab brown curtains of his apartment, stood a familiar silhouette.

"Shit," Tess said. "Drink up fast, kid."

"What's the matter?"

"Your dad's home early. And I just realized I've probably broken some parental rule about right-before-dinner snacks."

"He's not going to care about a bunch of milk. It's got calcium." Rosie slurped loudly. "He'll probably be more upset about me ending up in the school office."

"You don't have anything to worry about—you were a mere bystander." Tess maneuvered into a parking space. "I'm the one who blew it."

"Jared Medvedev said you kicked Mrs. Stanton's butt."

"Yeah, I did—and it needed to be kicked—but it was still a waste of time." She switched off the ignition, picked up her toffee-and-vanilla latte and sipped. "You've got to pick your battles. That's what Mémère always says."

"What's a *mémère?*"

"A scary old lady. I'd tell you more about her, but you're too young. I don't want to give you nightmares. Come on, drink up," Tess said as she leaned toward her window and peered at the third floor. "I think we've been spotted."

"Is that what you do with my dad?" Rosie asked. "Pick your battles?"

"Your dad's an exception to that rule." Actually, Quinn was turning out to be an exception to every rule Tess had in her playbook. "I've decided dealing with him requires a different strategy."

She shifted to face Quinn's daughter. "With your dad, everything's a battle. Everything we discuss—no matter how small, no matter how big—is something to hit him over the head with. Wear him down, that's what I'm going to do. Grind him down to a little nub of no resistance." She rubbed her thumb and fingers together. "That's my strategy. This is an all-out war to get that building done the way I want it done, and I'm going to win."

Rosie shook her head. "I'm not so sure about that."

"Why? Don't you think I've got what it takes?"

"Probably." Rosie finished her shake and wiped her mouth with the back of her hand. "But you don't know my dad. He's stubborn."

"I'm stubborner."

Rosie dragged her pack into her lap. "My mom says my dad is like one of those big rocks off shore. Storms and surf beating at him all the time, and he just sits there and takes it."

"Sounds boring. And annoying."

"Tell me about it," Rosie said. She grabbed the door handle and then paused to look back at Tess. "Have you won an argument with him yet?"

"Sure."

The kid gave her a skeptical frown. "Really?"

"Of course."

Tess set down her cup. There was an important point to be made here, and now that the kid was talking again, she wanted to keep the conversation on track. "But that's not the point. He's the exception to the rule, remember? Mémère's philosophy is that looking for a fight all the time makes a person mean and petty. And in spite of what Jared Medvedev said, the fight I picked today ended up making me feel mean and petty and stupid. It made me lose my cool, which I really hate. Shrewish isn't one of my better looks."

Tess checked her reflection in the rearview mirror and fluffed her hair, waiting to see if the kid had anything to say.

Rosie toyed with the handle. "Do you ever wish you could stop fighting with him?"

"With your dad? If I quit, I wouldn't know what to do with him. Confrontation is the basis of our relationship."

Rosie slowly sank back against her seat and stared through the windshield. "Do you like him?"

"I do. In a narrowly defined version of the term 'like,' that is."

"Even when you're fighting with him?"

"Especially when I'm fighting with him." Tess took a fortifying sip of her cooling latte. "Let me tell you something about your dad. Even when he's just plain wrong and I want to bash in his pigheaded face, he's still a pretty awesome guy. I'll share this secret—and you have to swear you won't tell him I said this, or I swear, I'll kick your butt—I actually admire him."

"Yeah, but, do you…" Rosie fingered the strap on her pack. "You know, do you like, *like* him?"

"You mean, the girl-guy kind of like?"

"Yeah."

"Now there's a loaded question," Tess said. "With all sorts of answers, depending on the context. Don't worry, kid," she added when Rosie gave her the stink eye. "I'm not going to duck out on this, although I wish I hadn't started it."

She took a deep breath. "Yes, I find your dad extremely sexy."

"Eeuww."

"Hey," Tess said. "You asked. If you don't want to hear the answer, don't ask the question."

Rosie gave her a suspicious, sideways glance. "How come you're talking to me like this?"

"Like what?"

"Telling me all this stuff."

"Why wouldn't I? If I don't want to answer one of your questions, I'll just tell you to mind your own business. It's called conversation, kid, remember? People do it all the time." She took another sip. "Besides, talking to you is kind of interesting. I wonder if you'd keep me interested past the first few dates."

"Girls don't go on dates."

"Yes, they do. I go out on girl dates with my girl-friends all the time." She took another sip. "What do you think this was?"

"You just picked me up from school."

"Hey, we kicked some butt, we got some snacks. We've been stuck together in this car for half an hour." Tess tilted her head back and drained the last of the coffee. "That's longer than some of my dates have lasted."

"Time for me to go."

"Rosie."

The kid climbed from the car and then turned to face her. "Yeah?"

"You're not going to tell your dad I think he's sexy, are you?"

"Puh-leeze." Rosie rolled her eyes as she slammed the door.

Tess waited until she walked into her building. And then she leaned her head against her window and glanced at the figure staring down at her from the third floor. "She's not so bad, Quinn. Fiesty, but I can relate."

CHAPTER FIFTEEN

TESS PERCHED on a stool at the wide kitchen island at Chandler House late Saturday afternoon. With the sun peeking below the awning and Aretha on the radio, Tess was certain there were no problems in the world that couldn't be solved with a plate of Julia's snickerdoodles and a tall glass of ice-cold milk. She'd figured out the answers to plenty of life's questions in this particular spot. So she was certain that if she concentrated hard enough—and ate enough cookies—she could figure out what to do about Quinn, too.

Not that she wanted to do anything about him except hold on tight and enjoy the ride for as long as it lasted. She'd had a week to calm down and think things through after her flight from his apartment, and now she knew what she wanted: an affair. With him. And since her usual method of handling an affair—comfortable boundaries and a casual distance—had worked every time in the past, she reassured herself it would probably work again this time. Boundaries would be important with Quinn.

Distance would be essential with his kid.

So now that she had things figured out, all neat and tidy, why was her stomach looping in knots, and why were so many cookie crumbs catching in her throat? She grabbed for her glass.

"What time did you say Miss Addie and that fool Charlie were getting here?" Julia rolled her marble pin across a sheet of pastry dough. "I want to get this pie in the oven before I head to town."

Tess glanced at the clock fixed to the wall above the big steel-fronted refrigerators. "Any minute now. And why is Charlie a fool?"

"I've seen her beau. Any woman who would drag her feet about marrying a man like that needs her head examined."

"She loves Jack. She just isn't looking forward to getting dressed up and having everyone stare at her." Both concepts were completely alien to Tess, but she'd stick up for Charlie because she was a loyal friend.

Loyal to a fault, as Mémère was fond of reminding her.

"Then they should have decided to elope," Julia said.

"She suggested that, but Jack doesn't want to sneak away. He says he wants plenty of witnesses so she can't back out of the deal later." Tess sipped her milk. "He also says he wants to watch her walk down the aisle to him."

"With a scowl on her face, most likely."

"Probably." Tess smiled. "Definitely." She set an elbow on the counter, rested her chin in her hand and sighed. "I think it's romantic."

"The words *romantic* and *Charlie Keene* don't exactly match up too well, do they?" Julia asked.

Tess smiled around the rim of her glass as she finished her milk. She wondered if all these doubters—herself included—would dissolve in tears at the sight of Charlie in white, clutching a fistful of flowers.

Julia draped the pastry over one of her wide pie dishes and began to fill it with shaved apple slices. "It's been too long since Miss Addie came around for a visit. I miss her."

"Well, you'll get to see both of them now." Tess scooted off the stool at the sound of a car in the drive beyond the kitchen door. "They said they'd meet me here."

Julia wiped her flour-dusted hands on her apron. "They'll be wanting some of my cookies."

"Why do you think they told me to meet them in the kitchen?"

A few moments later, Julia had her arms around "her girls" and was offering cookies and milk, just like old times.

Addie pulled out a stool next to Tess, and Charlie slouched against the island across from them. "Mm-mm," Charlie said as she bit into a snickerdoodle. "Let's skip those fancy frosted cakes and have these at the wedding."

"Snickerdoodles on the south lawn." Julia shook her head as she slid her pie into the oven. "Miz Geneva would never recover."

Charlie licked a milk mustache from her upper lip. "A couple dozen of these might make a nice wedding present."

"I can do better than that," Julia said.

"Okay. How about a couple dozen every week for a year?"

"Enough about the cookies." Tess pulled a notepad from her tote. "How about the cake?"

"Ooh, the cake. I've got some pictures." Addie rummaged through her scuffed, sagging tote and hefted a thick pile of bridal magazines onto the counter.

"Not the magazines." Charlie shoved her milk aside and buried her face in her crossed arms. "Anything but the magazines."

"Let me see, sweetie." Julia slid onto the stool next

to Addie and opened a bloated magazine bristling with sticky markers. "Now, isn't that pretty?"

"We could use fresh flowers to decorate the tops of the layers," Addie said. "Fresh flowers would work, wouldn't they?"

"They add a nice touch." Tess licked her fingers and craned her neck to peer at the photo over Addie's shoulder. "I like the way those are draped and swirled over the edges. What do you think, Charlie?"

"I think I want another snickerdoodle." She crossed the kitchen to the oversize bin near the cooktop.

Julia set the oven's timer. "I'm leaving you in charge, Miss Addie. You see that this pie gets pulled out and set on the rack when that buzzer goes off, or you're going to have me to answer to."

"Yes, ma'am." Addie grinned as Julia lightly flicked her arm with a tea towel.

"All right. Let's get down to business," Tess said when Julia had gone. She opened her notepad and clicked a pen. "Where do we start? Cake? Flowers? We should probably start with the flowers, because— What?" she asked when she saw the look that passed between Charlie and Addie.

"I heard you got sent to the principal's office at Adams Elementary School," Charlie said.

"Oh, that. That's not exactly what happened." Tess tried to wave it off, but Charlie crossed her arms and rested on the island, settling in to hear the whole sordid tale. "How did you hear about it?" Tess asked.

"Jason Cardoza's mother was dropping off some flyers at the school office," Charlie told her.

"And who is Jason Cardoza?"

"One of the boys on Jack's Little League team."

Tess narrowed her eyes. "Sometimes I think this town's grapevine needs some serious pruning."

"What we want to know is, what were you doing at the school?" Addie asked.

"Picking up Quinn's daughter."

"Hmm." Charlie gave Addie another of those annoying looks. "Interesting."

"There was nothing 'interesting' about it," Tess said. "I was doing him a favor. That's all."

"You're turning red." Addie studied her over the rim of her glass. "You wouldn't be turning red if it was just a favor."

"Maybe she's been doing other favors for Quinn." Charlie wiggled her eyebrows. "Favors we don't know about. Yet."

"We could ask her," Addie suggested.

"I have an idea," Tess said as she stood and gathered her things. "Why don't we continue this interrogation outside. You can plan for the wedding and torture me at the same time."

"Okay." Charlie straightened and headed toward the door leading to the back hall. "Dibs on the thumbscrews."

"We can't go outside yet," Addie said. "I have to wait for the pie. And we don't mean to torture you," she told Tess. "We're just curious about what's going on between you and Quinn."

"What makes you think something's going on? What?" Tess asked. "There's that look again. Stop giving each other that look."

"What look?" Addie asked.

"The we-know-she's-hiding-something-from-us look."

"Guilty as charged." Charlie returned and swung up on one of the stools. "So—what are you hiding from us?"

Tess tried staring them down, but she was outnumbered. "All right, all right. For crying out loud." She inhaled deeply and blew out a put-upon sigh. "There was…this…kiss."

"I knew it." Charlie slapped the counter. "I knew there was something going on the night you two came over for dinner."

"Just a kiss?" Addie asked.

"You sound so disappointed," Tess said.

"She's not." Charlie shook her head. "I'm not. It's just that we're a little worried about you. Usually you're…"

"Getting more than kisses?" Tess asked.

"Happier." Addie ran her hand down Tess's arm. "Aren't you happy, Tess?"

It was the reassuring, uncomplicated gesture that did Tess in—the contrast between the sweet simplicity of that touch and the terrifying complications casting shadows over her personal life.

"I don't know." Tess swallowed, mortified by the sting behind her eyes and the burn in her throat. "I don't know what's going on, what's going to happen between Quinn and me. I want an affair, but I know it'll be painful and messy—there's no avoiding it."

"Are you sure?" Addie asked.

"He's an alcoholic," Tess said. "He's got a kid. I'm working with him. How much worse could it be?"

"He could be married," Charlie pointed out.

Tess huffed out a shaky laugh. "You're right. Things could be worse. But I don't do those things. I don't do messy and painful. So I've been asking myself why don't I just give up on the idea?"

"Because he kissed you," Addie said.

"Yes, he did." Tess shivered, remembering. "He kissed me. I mean, he *kissed* me, and omigod, I want him. I'm scared to death how much I want him. There," she said, glaring at her friends. "Are you satisfied now? Totally-in-control, love-'em-and-leave-'em Tess Roussel has been brought to her knees by a moody, troubled man, with just one kiss."

"Must have been some kiss," Charlie said.

"Take my word for it." Tess sucked in a deep breath and let it out slowly. "The man may have his faults—and plenty of them—but he knows how to kiss."

ON SUNDAY AFTERNOON Quinn sat in the local minor league field bleachers with his daughter and a crowd of people he barely knew. He drank lukewarm lemonade, watched his newest crew member strike out twice in the first four innings and listened to Tess's low-level whining about the sticky seat, the flat soda, the rude couple two rows down and the high price of the sandals she wanted for a new dress. He closed his eyes, tipped his head back and let the sun warm his face.

Life was good.

He still couldn't believe he was here, instead of checking the equipment at the job site. But he'd thought Rosie might enjoy the outing. And when Mick and Jack had ganged up on him to twist both arms—not-so-subtly pointing out that Tess would be here, too—he'd agreed to help with the chaperoning duties for Jack's Little League team.

Tess jostled his elbow as she scooted her feet out of the aisle, scrunching back and turning her face to the side to avoid a nose-to-butt-crack encounter with the fan heading to an empty seat farther down their row. "Gee, Quinn. You sure know how to show a girl a good time."

"I'm having fun." Behind them, Addie noisily slurped the last of her soda and then yelled at the ump. "I haven't seen a Wildcats game in years. I forgot how exciting it can be."

"Glad you're enjoying it." Quinn stole a handful of popcorn from Tess's bag and shoved it into his mouth.

"Don't get too impressed with yourself." Tess brushed a stray fleck of popcorn from her light blue pants. "Addie doesn't get out much."

The batter caught one high and inside, sending a pop fly into left field. Addie gripped Tess's shoulder as Mick went deep, deep, loping into position and making the catch look as easy as pie.

"He's wonderful," Addie said. "And incredibly cute."

"Think so?" Tess leaned forward, giving Mick a squinting once-over. "Quinn can introduce you after the game."

"No," Quinn said.

"Why not?" Tess dug into her bag and pulled out two fluffy kernels. "He's single. Addie's single. And she's right—he is sort of cute."

"Bad combination," Quinn said.

"I thought you liked him."

"I hired him. I'm not going to date him."

"I'm not going to date him, either," Addie said. "Unless he asks me."

"You don't know anything about him." Quinn stared into the outfield with a frown. "He might be lying about being single. He could be a bigamist with a wife in every town he's ever lived in."

"What's a bigamist?" Rosie asked.

"A man who's married to more than one woman at a

time," Tess told her. "Which is something Mick could never afford on what your dad's paying him."

"He doesn't look like a bigamist." Addie jumped to her feet to boo with the crowd.

"What does a bigamist look like?" Rosie asked.

"Like any other man. Which is one reason they're so scary." Tess reached across Quinn to offer Rosie some popcorn. "Bigamists, I mean. Men aren't scary at all."

After a slight hesitation, Rosie took one piece.

Quinn silently released the breath he'd been holding. *Progress.* After Tess had picked Rosie up from school on Wednesday, Rosie had refused to tell him what had happened in the office or what she and Tess had discussed during the time they'd spent together. She'd been unusually subdued the rest of the week—not with her usual sullen silence, but with a considering sort of quiet.

Whatever Tess had accomplished with his daughter, Quinn wished she'd do it again. He glanced at her profile, enjoying her nearness, wishing he could hold her sticky hand. Instead, he took his daughter's hand and gave it a quick squeeze.

Rosie squeezed back.

Quinn froze, afraid to let go but afraid to hold on a moment too long. Addie jumped up behind them again, cheering another of Mick's plays and the end of the inning, nudging his arm with her knee. Rosie's hand slipped from his.

"Can I get you something?" he asked her. *Anything. Right now, I'll try to get you anything in the world you want.*

"Nah." His daughter sucked her soda through a straw as obnoxiously as Addie had done. Quinn caught her eyeing one of Jack's Little Leaguers, who happened to look back at the same time and then duck his head shyly. "I'm fine," she said.

God. Maybe he shouldn't have left her alone with Tess after all.

SHORTLY AFTER 3:00 p.m. on Friday, Rosie plopped her ten-year-old butt on the passenger seat of Tess's roadster and hauled her backpack onto her lap. Her it's-an-ordeal sigh made it clear that everything—the end of the school day, Tess's arrival, the weight of the books and homework assignments in the bag—was part of a plot to rob her of any chance of happiness. "This is getting to be a bad habit," she said when she'd slammed her door.

"Tell me about it." Tess blew a kiss at the Stepford cop as she pulled out of the appropriate pick-up spot and joined the orderly line of appropriate family vehicles waiting to proceed at the appropriate snail's pace to the exit. "I've got better things to do on a Friday afternoon."

"Like what?"

"Like getting ready for Friday night."

"What's wrong?" the kid asked with sweetly innocent concern. "Having problems with your cable hookup?"

"Ha. Ha." Tess spared her a miserly grin. "Score one for the whippersnapper."

Rosie sighed again and fiddled with the strap on her bag. "Is my dad going to be home in time for dinner?"

"Don't count on it. The delivery they were expecting this morning got pushed back to this afternoon, and the crew is working overtime to get everything stored and secured before the weekend hits. Why?"

Rosie heaved another martyr's sigh. "Nothing."

"Hey. I'm a girl. I know when 'nothing' means nothing and when it means everything." Tess downshifted to ease around a corner. "Talk to me, kid."

Rosie's shrug was sharp and unhappy. "There's nothing you can do about it."

"Try me."

Rosie chewed on her lower lip and stared out the windshield. Tess figured she was weighing her desire to get what she wanted against her need to punish Tess for existing.

Desire won out. "I'm invited to a party tonight," she said. "A birthday party."

"Get out." Tess braked for a signal and stared at her. "You've got friends?"

"Ha. Ha. Score one for the forty-year-old with the bags under her eyes."

"Thirty-one. And amazingly wrinkle-free."

"Must be the lighting."

Enjoying the conversation more than she'd expected she might, Tess made her turn through the intersection. "About this party…"

"Alana's mother told her she had to invite all the girls in the class." Rosie began to shred a different portion of her lip. "Dad hasn't taken me shopping to buy the present yet."

"Men."

"Yeah."

"What are you wearing?" Tess asked.

Rosie glanced at her dingy white T-shirt and khaki cargo pants. "What do you mean?"

"To the party." Tess checked Rosie's mouth to see whether she'd drawn blood. "Every girl in your class is going to be there, right?"

"Yeah. So?"

"So, this is an opportunity to make a major fashion statement. In an entirely not-the-usual-school-clothes way."

"What's wrong with what I have on?" Rosie pointed at the baggy pants and worn athletic shoes. "All I have to pack is some pajamas and another shirt for tomorrow."

"An overnight?" Tess shuddered at the thought of a class full of young girls camped in one house through the endless hours of a slumber party. Alana's mother must be a saint. Or on some really powerful drugs. "Triple the fashion play."

"Triple?"

"There's the arrival outfit. The pajama scene. And the morning after. Three chances to make a statement."

"I don't want to make a statement." Rosie slumped in her seat. "I probably can't go, anyway."

"I don't see why not. You got the invitation, right? And it's not like you've got anything else to do tonight except wait around for your dad to get home."

Another jerky, dismissive shrug.

"Besides," Tess said, "every woman wants to make a statement. And if you're wearing the coolest clothes in the room, you don't have to open your mouth to do it."

No response. Misery hung in the car's air-conditioned atmosphere, a miasma of heartache and despair.

And memories.

With a sad and resigned sigh of her own, Tess checked her watch before pulling her car's phone set from her purse and hooking it to her ear. "Quinn, it's me. Yeah, I made the pickup, no problem. Just wanted to let you know I'm going to run a few errands… With Rosie, right. And it's going to cost you." Tess wiggled her eyebrows at the kid. "Seems there's a birthday party in the works… Yeah, that's what I figured. No problem. I'll take care of it. Just promise you'll pay me back."

Tess handed Rosie the phone. "He wants to talk to you."

She listened in while Rosie gave her dad a surly dose of grief and guilt and then cut in when she figured Quinn had suffered enough. "Remind him he said he'd pay me back," she said. "And tell him it's going to be expensive."

The kid's face brightened as she relayed the message, and Tess's initial plan began to sprout multileveled additions and extravagant decor.

"He wants to know how much," Rosie said.

"Enough to feel the pinch, but not enough to dip into your college savings." Tess changed direction and headed toward the mall—it was the simplest solution to spending money on a tight schedule. "I'm not that irresponsible."

Rosie extended the phone toward her. "Your turn."

"Now what?" Tess asked Quinn. "Oh. Yeah. That's right." She glanced at the kid—the primary stumbling block to an affair, the complication who was about to be disposed of for an entire evening. Tess's attitude toward her upcoming errands improved dramatically. "No, I— Look," she told Quinn, her face heating, "we'll discuss the details later. Got to go."

Tess fumbled as she slipped the phone back into her tote, her pulse stuttering as she considered Quinn's suggestion.

"What's the matter?" Rosie asked.

"Nothing."

"Your face is all red." The kid's eyes narrowed in a suspicious squint. "Looks like that 'nothing' means something."

"Here we are." Tess pulled into the compact parking

area beside her favorite salon, effectively changing the subject. "Hop out."

"This isn't a place to buy a present."

"No, but it's a place to get ready for a Friday night." A Friday night with a single father who had realized he was going to be free for the evening. A single man who had asked her out to dinner.

A gorgeous man whose low, husky-voiced invitation had included a few suggestions for what would probably follow the meal.

CHAPTER SIXTEEN

TESS USHERED Rosie through the pink-trimmed doors of Shear Delight and led her to one of the styling stations. "Hey, Jana," she said, resting a hand on the kid's shoulder. "I brought you a new customer. This is Rosie Quinn. Any chance you can squeeze her in?"

Jana swept the floor and smiled as she gave Rosie a discreet once-over. "Are we doing a trim or a style?"

"I'm thinking a few layers." Tess circled Rosie, imagining the sweep and fall of that thick black hair once it had been freed from its plain elastic band. "Maybe some bangs to frame her face, bring out her eyes."

"They're beautiful eyes." Jana's smile widened as she gestured toward the chair. "What do you think, pretty Rosie? Should we make you even prettier?"

Two bright pink spots flared on the kid's cheeks. "I don't know if I'm supposed to get my hair cut."

"If you're worried about your dad, don't be," said Tess. "I'll call him and take care of it."

Jana opened a magazine on her work counter and flipped to a page filled with girlish styles. "What do you think?"

"I like this one." Rosie pointed to a photo of a young girl whose hair was caught up with loose braids.

"That would be great for the party," Tess agreed.

"A party?" Jana fastened the drape around Rosie's neck and gently removed the elastic. "Then we'll have to do something extra special."

Rosie stared at her reflection, digging into her lower lip as if it were an entrée. "Would it look just like the picture?"

Tess pulled out her phone. "Quinn? We need you to make a fashion decision. Bangs and layers or just— Yeah, okay. Right."

She dropped her phone back into her tote. "Anything you want, kid."

Rosie's shy smile spread until it brightened the room. "I want to look like the picture in the magazine."

"You heard the lady," Tess said with a wide smile of her own. "Give her the works."

BY THE TIME Quinn limped through his apartment door at exactly eight minutes after seven o'clock, his system was buzzing on caffeine, painkillers, temper and nerves. An idiot inspector had him considering a new career, he'd twisted his knee tripping over a pipe, Tess had him wondering whether he'd be able to pay this month's rent, Rosie was probably planning on a weeklong silent treatment and his cravings for a cold beer and hot tobacco threatened to send him to his aching, creaking knees. "Rosie?"

"In here," Tess called.

He headed down the short hall and turned toward Rosie's room. Tess hadn't sounded upset the last time they'd spoken—good. Or bad, if the source of that cheery greeting had been a shopping spree he'd still be paying off when Christmas hit. "Rosie, I'm—"

He froze in the doorway, and all his aches and resentments and frustrations and despair drained through the soles of his mud-caked boots. Tess knelt on Rosie's floor, her back to him, laying expertly folded pajamas into an open suitcase. The pajamas were neon-pink, dotted with bright palm trees and goofy flamingos, and new. Beside her lay a pair of fat, pink, pig-shaped slippers, also new.

And then his daughter stepped forward. With her hair pinned up in some sort of fancy twist and soft black wisps framing her big dark eyes, and her face alight with hope and blushing with shyness, the worst of Quinn's day completely evaporated.

"Rosie," he said. The word came out like a croak, and he had to pause, struggling to swallow to get the next words out. "You're a picture."

"Isn't she, though?" Tess stretched toward Rosie's bed and lifted another folded outfit off the spread. "My stylist says her bone structure is classic. She's going to be a beauty, Quinn. You're going to have to keep a club handy to beat back the boys when she's ready to date. And doesn't that outfit show off her coloring?"

"Yes," he said, though he hadn't been able to pry his gaze from his daughter's face.

Tess continued to babble about the opinions of a bunch of women at some beauty parlor, but Quinn could only stare at Rosie, afraid to move, afraid to speak. He was in for it now, he thought as her eyes brimmed with tears. First, he'd been late and now he was obviously not offering the right kind of praise. And he'd wanted to, damn it. He'd wanted to say exactly what Rosie needed to hear. There she stood, looking like something out of a dream, and he desperately wanted to be whatever she needed him to be.

She rushed toward him and threw her arms around

his waist and pressed one side of her face against his shirt. His arms came up, and his big, clumsy hands flexed and trembled and then settled on her thin shoulders. He glanced at Tess, awkward with panic, and then his vision blurred, and he curled around his daughter and hid his face against her soft hair. She smelled of shampoo and flowers and the stuff women smell of when they'd been hanging around each other. "Rosie," he whispered.

"Looks like I'm finished here," Tess said, and then she slipped from the room and quietly shut the door behind her.

FIFTEEN MINUTES LATER, Tess paced before the tall window in Quinn's front room, chewing on her thumb. Nasty habit, but she figured she could cut herself some slack after the afternoon she'd had. Her leisurely weekend-prep program—maintenance trim, soothing pedicure, lingerie sale browsing—had turned into a frenzied preteen makeover. Fun but exhausting. And a bit nerve-racking, considering the preteen involved wasn't her own.

She'd already decided that if Quinn complained about the afternoon's expenses, she'd offer to lump that discussion in with their next battle over specs. It was about time to toss him a negotiation point. Or two.

"Time to go," she said as Quinn and his daughter entered the room. "It's okay to be fashionably late, but if you don't get started soon you'll edge into the rude zone. Got the present?"

"Wait'll you see it, Dad." Rosie dashed down the hall.

"Don't forget to sign the card," Tess called after her. "And write a little note, off to the side, not just your name."

Quinn slid his hands into his pockets and stood where he was, an unreadable expression on his face.

"Well." Tess cleared her throat and gestured toward the table. "There's the invitation. You'll need it for the address."

He nodded. "Thank you."

"My pleasure. The shopping part—not the kid."

"I hope she behaved."

"She behaved the way she's supposed to. Like a ten-year-old girl with a lot of problems." Tess shrugged. "They're not my problems. I'm not the one who has to live with her."

"Tess." Rosie raced back into the room holding a big card and a small package. "I don't know how to attach the card to the box."

"With tape. Stick it to the bottom of the box."

"Just a second." The kid took off toward her room again.

"Where would you like to go to dinner?" Quinn asked.

Tess swept back her bangs, hiding her nerves. "I may have exaggerated my responsibility with your budget. The college savings are still intact, but you can't afford dinner."

"Can I afford a pizza?"

"How about I whip up something quick and easy at my place?"

"Okay," he said, his gaze smoldering. "I'm easy. Whipping sounds good."

TESS CURSED the tremor in her hand as she lit the single taper in the middle of her intimate table setting. She never got nervous fixing dinner for a man—and she definitely didn't get nervous merely thinking about it.

Maybe it wasn't the dinner, she thought as she waved

the match to extinguish the flame. Maybe it was what she knew would come after the main course.

She pressed a hand to her stomach to soothe the flutters of anticipation—and nerves, damn it. What was it about Quinn that cut through her composure and set her knees knocking?

After she'd had her way with him, she'd put him in his place and keep him there. She'd been too understanding lately. Too cooperative. Too sympathetic over his problems with his daughter and his worries about his crew. Too eager to compromise and avoid any unpleasantness between them that might add to his troubles. Just look at the fabulous dinner she'd tossed together so he could relax and unwind at her home instead of having to take her out on the town.

And what a dinner it would be. She returned to her kitchen to stir her soup and sniffed the rich aroma of caramelized onions and herbs. Perfect. And peeked at the marinated pork tenderloin roasting in the oven before lowering the temperature to warm. Excellent. And admired the spiral pattern of the potato gratin cooling on the rack. Gorgeous. Simple food, basics she'd found in her refrigerator, done up in style.

Too bad she was too nervous to consider eating a bite.

Her stirring spoon clattered to the floor when she heard the knock on the door. He was earlier than she'd expected. Eager for the evening to start, no doubt. She paused by the little mirror in her entry, fussing with the drape of her off-the-shoulder sweater and smoothing a hand over her slit-hemmed capris before glancing down at her darling new ribboned slides. Lifting her chin and giving her reflection one of her coolest smiles, she took a deep breath and pulled open her door.

And melted into a mess of fluttering goo when she saw the huge bunch of soft blue irises in Quinn's hand.

"I would have brought you roses," he said, thrusting the flowers at her with a stiffly awkward arm, "but you seemed to like these."

He'd had his hair trimmed, and there was a reddened nick near the dent on his chin where he must have cut himself shaving. His navy-blue oxford shirt was tucked into a pair of tan trousers, his scuffed dress shoes were freshly polished, and the way he looked at her made her feel as if she was the most beautiful woman he'd ever seen.

The flutters intensified, and she swallowed to ease the strange tightness in her throat. "I do. They're beautiful, Quinn. Thank you."

She took the fat bouquet and stepped aside as he entered, and then closed the door. "Let me get a—"

He wrapped an arm around her waist, fisted a hand in her hair, shoved her against the wall and took her mouth in a kiss that flashed through her like wildfire. The flowers tumbled to the floor at their feet as she twined her arms around his neck and plastered herself against him, punishing him with her lips and teeth and battling for control as her system rocketed toward arousal at light speed.

"I want you," he murmured against her throat.

"I can tell," she said on a gasp as his tongue blazed a moist trail along the base of her throat.

"Now," he said.

She tugged at the buttons on his shirt, and he yanked at her sweater, tugging the hem above her bra, lifting her arms above her head, imprisoning her wrists in thick manacles of cashmere while his mouth ravished hers. Holding her there, pinned to the wall, he stroked a long, callus-roughened hand down her center to her waistband and fumbled with the zipper closing while those hot blue eyes of his locked on hers.

"Let me go," she said.

"Not a chance." But he tore the sweater from her hands and flung it to the floor. She kicked off her shoes and reached again for his shirt buttons, popping one loose as she struggled to slip it through its hole, abandoning her efforts when he slapped her hands aside and ripped the rest of it wide. She slid his belt through its buckle and undid the catch above his zipper while his hands streaked behind her to undo the fastening on her bra. He yanked the straps down her arms, baring her breasts, and then he lowered his head and sucked one nipple deep within his mouth.

She moaned and arched into him, grabbing fistfuls of his hair, fighting to drag breath into her burning lungs. She battled to keep her balance as he ground his hips against hers, lifting her off the floor, her back to the wall and his solid, muscular body at her front.

The scents of aftershave and flowers, roasting meat and salt-tinged skin overwhelmed her. The sounds of labored breathing and desperate whimpers and limbs crashing against the wall beat in counterpoint to her beating heart. And the contrasts of coarse hair and smooth flesh and dizzying panic began to spiral through her.

"Not here," she said.

"Not enough."

He bent and scooped her into his arms and strode through the front room toward the darkened hall. When he found her room at the end of it he lowered her to the bed and followed her down, sprawling over her, shoving one leg between hers and clamping his mouth over her breast.

She bowed up, urging him to the side, and rolled with him. Rising over him, she fought with the zipper on his pants as he reached up to take her by the arms and drag her down. Down, down to his ravening mouth, to those dark and delicious kisses, her nipples rubbing over his chest with a tingling, scorching friction as his tongue swept through her mouth and his hands kneaded her hips.

"Pants," he murmured against her mouth.

"Off," she said as she struggled to her side and wrestled her waistband down her hips, clumsy with haste. The faint crackle of tinfoil, the list and lurch of the mattress beneath his weight, and then he was on her again, his hands rough and shaking as he slid the last barrier of silk down her legs. His fingers found her, wet and ready for him, and she wrapped her arms around his neck and raked her fingers down his broad, quivering back as he stroked her, hard and fast and wild. Too fast, too much, too soon.

She kicked out, and her bedside lamp toppled and crashed as she angled back, squirming beneath him. His big, heavy body shifted and stretched over hers, and he settled between her legs, and those rugged, workman's hands gathered her close.

"Quinn."

"Yes."

He cradled her head in his hands as he plunged inside her, and though she couldn't see his face in the shadows, she knew he was watching her, staring intently, looking through her with his piercing gaze. She wondered if he could see what she was feeling, what she wanted from him—things she couldn't understand. And then, as if he knew exactly what they were, he began to move in long, deep strokes, touching her in places she hadn't realized anyone could.

She arched again, straining for one final, agonizing, glorious moment on the keen edge between anticipation and abandon. And then the world exploded in strobes of sheet lightning and pounding thunder and sensation and Quinn's hoarse, ragged cry as he tensed and pistoned into her.

QUINN LAY motionless, staring at the shadows rippling across Tess's ceiling, one arm crooked beneath his head and the other resting across her long, narrow waist. Her hair tickled his chin, but he was afraid to move. Afraid if he did move, she'd stop running her fingernails in teasing circles around one of his nipples, or pull her soft thigh from the top of his, or shift away from his side. Or that she'd climb out of bed and leave him behind in the rumpled spread he'd pulled over them to form an intimate cocoon.

He couldn't remember the last time he'd felt the comforting weight of another body pressed like this against him, the gentle heat of a woman's skin against his. Right now, he thought it had to be the best feeling in the world.

Well, the second best, anyway.

"I hope you like overcooked meat and cold potatoes," Tess said.

"My favorites."

"Good. That's what I made for dinner."

He stroked his hand down her spine. A long, elegant sweep. The womanly flare of hip, the incredible curves beyond. "I'm sure it's great."

"Mmm." She leaned up to press a soft kiss to his cheek. "Like the sex."

He froze. He hadn't thought of what they'd shared as sex. He'd been making love to her. Clumsily, perhaps, as eager and impatient as a schoolboy, but with as much affection as he could safely convey.

Anything more would have spelled disaster, for both of them.

He skimmed his fingers up into her hair. "Sex happens to be another of my favorites."

She sighed and snuggled closer. "I hate to move from this particular spot, but I should be a better hostess and not keep you waiting for your meal."

"No complaints about the hostess so far." He moved his hand from her waist to her breast. "I wouldn't mind skipping dinner and going straight to the dessert course."

"Tempting." She rose on one elbow. "I find you very tempting, Quinn."

"Same goes."

"I don't suppose you'd be interested in an affair."

He should have expected the up-front talk. He should have been grateful she was the one doing the asking— any man in his place would have been thrilled. But her suggestion—and his reaction to it—annoyed him. "I'd be willing to consider it," he said.

She stilled, and he hoped he hadn't offended her.

"It's hard for you, isn't it?" she asked a few moments later. "With Rosie, I mean."

Rosie. He hadn't given her a thought during the past hour. And now that she was suddenly there again, between them, he wanted to share her with Tess.

His daughter had been full of Tess on the drive to the party. Where Tess had taken her shopping, what Tess had said about her hair, how Tess had dropped hints about her wardrobe, why Tess had suggested the charm bracelet for Alana's gift.

He wanted to ask Tess whether she thought Rosie would like a similar bracelet for a Christmas present. He wanted to know if she liked his daughter. If she thought she might find a way to someday, somehow, care for Rosie.

If there was going to be two women in his life, it would be damn difficult to keep them separate. He didn't want his daughter to be just another item to consider when discussing the logistics of a love affair. But if they were going to have an affair—and he desperately wanted to—the subject of Rosie was bound to come up.

He sighed with a mix of confusion and guilt. "Single fatherhood does tend to complicate things. Not that I've had all that many offers for an affair lately."

"We can figure something out, I suppose." Tess stood and righted her lamp on a bedside table. "If you want to."

"Tess." He sat up, extended a hand and waited until she placed hers into it. And then he tugged her down on the bed, cupped her chin and pressed a sweet, gentle kiss to her mouth. "I want you. More than ever."

Her fingers circled his wrist. "Same goes."

SHORTLY AFTER six the following morning, Quinn awoke in Tess's bed, his empty stomach complaining loudly. He stole a few minutes to stare at his lover, enjoying the sweep of her dark lashes over her curvy cheeks and the swell of her plump lower lip. In sleep, her features softened and relaxed, she looked younger, nearly delicate.

More beautiful than ever, and he hadn't thought that was possible.

His stomach rumbled again, and he eased from the bed, stepped into his jeans, slipped from her room and wandered through her house in search of the kitchen.

He'd made it as far as her bathroom last night, where they'd stumbled, laughing, to make love in her deep, cast-iron tub. And she'd escaped from his arms temporarily to tend to the remains of her dinner and carry crackers and cheese back to the bed for a midnight picnic on the sheets. But he'd been focused completely on her, and he hadn't noticed his surroundings.

Now, in the soft light of an early summer morning, her choices of paint and pattern hammered at his senses. A riot of jewel-bright colors burst from the French impressionist prints on her walls to flood her rooms with light and life. Flowers burst from vases and scented the rooms, and piles of fat pillows beckoned with promises of comfortable seating on curvy sofas and chairs. Sassy, whimsical touches—the orange glass crab crouching on a stack of books, the sad-eyed iron hound guarding a doorway—kept things casual.

Her personality enveloped him, and he stood silently and let it soak in like the sunshine beyond her windows.

He'd missed out on a good dinner, he discovered when he walked into her sunflower-yellow kitchen, saw the scraped pots and pans and caught a whiff of the lingering odors. And it appeared he'd miss out on breakfast, too, he discovered after checking her refrigerator and pantry.

He supposed he could run to the store for some cereal. His turn to do the cooking. He could bring her one of those candy-flavored coffees she drank by the gallon.

And he could detour past Tidewaters, check out the

site. Especially since he'd be making a late start on the job this morning.

If he got lucky, he wouldn't be starting the morning's chores until the afternoon.

QUINN NOTICED the jagged tear in the southern stretch of fencing at the job site before he'd completed his turn into the street.

And he smelled the leak before he spied the ugly edges of the cut lines. The stink of it hung in the air, heavy and sour, making his gut clench even before he'd spied the ominous stain spread over the damp ground. Hydraulic fluid. Gallons of it, he imagined, emptying from the tool carrier's tubes. And exactly how much this latest criminal assault on his equipment would cost in dollars and delays, he couldn't begin to imagine.

Rage roared through him, obliterating the spiraling despair before it could swamp him and take him down. He muttered a vicious curse as he tugged his phone from his pocket and hit an automatic-dial button. "Tess. Get down here."

She agreed and disconnected without asking any questions, and he was grateful she'd chosen not to press him for more information.

He squatted on his heels and stared at the ground beneath the tool carrier, careful to keep a safe distance from the edge of the spill. Whoever had done this had known exactly what to do, precisely how to deliver the most damage with the least effort. Quick, neat, efficient. Disable a vital piece of equipment. Tear up the site. Tie up the project for weeks—maybe months— during the cleanup. A cleanup that could cost hundreds of thousands, maybe millions of dollars. Guarantee

headlines that could turn public opinion against Tidewaters before it opened.

Rising, he stared at the shifting ripples of the bay.
And then he stooped to grab a fist-size stone and pitched
it with all his might and all his frustration and all his fury
into the gunmetal-gray water.

CHAPTER SEVENTEEN

TESS SIPPED her drive-through coffee, curling her hands around the hot cup and wishing the warmth of the drink could banish the icy dread layered beneath her skin.

A few yards away, Quinn huddled with the men who'd arrived in the police cruiser and the city vehicle and the county van and the state Department of Fish and Game truck. She had no idea how much longer they'd stand there, gesturing and making notes on clipboards. Or how much longer she'd have to wait for their decisions about Tidewaters' future.

Overhead, gulls swooped and jeered, their harsh voices grating on her nerves. Everything seemed brittle and cold this morning, although the sun was erasing the last of the morning mist ahead of schedule and the temperature was inching toward midsummer range.

She'd been so warm, so cozily content and relaxed a few hours ago, snuggled deep in her soft bed and wrapped tight in Quinn's embrace. So filled with drowsy what-ifs and dreamy plans, concerned with nothing more important than where to go for coffee and whether Quinn liked his eggs poached or scrambled.

She and Quinn should be in bed together right now, she thought with a pang of regret, scattering pastry crumbs in her sheets as they refueled for another session of lovemaking. Yet that lovely, soft-focus image seemed to blur and distort, as if she viewed it through a long, warped tunnel. At this moment, in this place, with the heavy odor of the spill tainting the sea air, the intimacies and whispers of last night seemed to have taken place years in the past.

Now she watched her lover prowl a wide perimeter around his vandalized equipment. His face was taut with worry and his eyes shadowed as he listened to the engineer from En-Tech. Were there signs of seepage near the southwest corner? They weren't discussing tearing down that bearing wall and digging out the foundation, were they?

She turned and stared at the building—their beautiful, wonderful building. Its pristine skeleton and patches of plywood skin, bright with promise in the sunlight, stood solid and secure a safe distance from the ugly smear on the ground.

It was a safe distance, wasn't it?

Quinn left the group behind and strode past her, headed toward his office trailer. "How are you doing?" he asked in a gruff, tight voice.

"Just for the record," she answered as she sipped at her drink, "I don't do mornings."

He paused, and a corner of his mouth lifted in the ghost of a smile. "Just for the record, it doesn't matter." And then he climbed the trailer steps and closed the door.

She could follow him. She could badger and pester and pry some more information out of him. He should have some more for her by now, considering how long he'd been in conference with the others. But she knew tests would have to be run, estimates made.

And she was afraid to learn the answers to her questions.

Geneva exited the Tidewaters building and slowly picked her way over the uneven ground to join Tess near the trailer. She glanced at her watch. "How much longer do you think this will take? I told Maudie I'd meet her for brunch today. We have wedding plans to discuss."

"Can you cancel?" Tess sipped again and then tugged her sweater around her middle and rubbed one hand along one arm. "I'm sure Maudie would understand."

"I don't see the need for all three of us to stay. And it appears that Quinn has matters under control." Geneva frowned as a voice crackled over the radio in the nearby patrol car. "As much as any of this can be under control, at any rate. Disgusting," she muttered. "Beyond contempt."

Tess shivered. "He can't stay. He'll need to pick up his daughter soon."

"Is she home alone?"

"No. She's at an overnight party."

"Couldn't he arrange for someone else to do it?" Geneva asked. "Couldn't you, perhaps?"

"No. He should be there for her. It's important for Rosie to—" Tess knew she'd said too much when her grandmother aimed a sharp, assessing look in her direction. "It's important," she finished lamely.

"I don't know whether to be pleased or dismayed that you're taking such an interest in your general contractor's personal life."

"He's not my contractor—he's yours. And don't trouble yourself on my account. Or his." Tess set her cup on her car's hood and shoved her hands into her sweater pockets. "It probably won't last long."

"No. It seems these things never do." Geneva held out her hand. "Loan me your phone, please, Tess dear, so I can arrange a later date with Maudie."

Geneva took the phone and wandered toward her car for some privacy, and Tess scowled and hunched her shoulders. She hated the way Mémère could make her feel as if she were five years old and covered with incriminating cookie crumbs. She was a grown woman, and if she chose to indulge in an affair, that was her decision to make. There was nothing wrong with enjoying the occasional adult relationship while she was waiting for the right circumstances and the right partner.

When she finally settled into marriage, it would be for all the right reasons—reasons that included the likelihood of financial stability and a suitably sophisticated groom. Someone who'd be a perfect match for her, in style and sensibilities. With no children thrown into the bargain. Getting used to having a man in her life would be tough enough without tripping over a smart-mouthed kid.

And if she was feeling a little wistful about the idea of Quinn going off by himself to pick up Rosie and hear all about the party…well, that was just part of the normal morning-after sentiment that was sometimes a by-product of the night before. It happened. Sometimes. Sort of.

Okay, not like this, maybe, but it was to be expected. It had been a long time since her last lover, and Quinn had been…exceptional.

She snapped out of her daydreamy mood as a green compact edged through the gate. "Shit."

Geneva returned the phone and nodded toward the approaching car. "Is that who I think it is?" she asked.

"It is if you think it's that Channel Six weasel Gregorio."

"I'm glad I stayed." Grandmère straightened and donned her regal attitude. "I believe I have a few things to say this morning, if Mr. Gregorio will be so kind as to listen. On the record," she added with a frosty smile.

GENEVA SET ASIDE Monday's edition of *The Cove Press* when Quinn walked into the Crescent Inn. He spoke to the cashier, nodded at her response and then strode down the aisle in Geneva's direction. Tall, athletic, purposeful—a rugged, good-looking man, a man who never asked more of his employees than he was willing to do himself. Very much like her own husband when she'd first met him, Geneva mused as he neared her table. "Good morning, Quinn."

"Good morning." He slid into the booth opposite her and murmured his thanks as he took the menu from Missy. "Thank you for meeting me this early," he told Geneva. "I seem to be making a habit of disturbing your mornings lately."

"I'm an early riser, and not much disturbs my sleep at my age."

She gave Missy her order and waited for Quinn to give his. After Missy had filled his coffee cup and left to see to the needs of another group across the room, Geneva leaned forward. "Let me begin our discussion by informing you that I intend to keep you on as my general contractor at Tidewaters. And that I also intend to see that building finished as my granddaughter designed it, no matter how long it takes or how much it costs."

"It might cost everything you've got."

She smiled tightly. "I have a great deal."

He settled against the booth's cushioned seat. "My insurer is getting nervous about my coverage. I can't promise I'll be able to keep my certificate."

"Which means the bank will withdraw its part in the financing." Geneva raised her cup to sip her tea. "And I'll be left to fund the entire project."

"That's a huge risk, considering what's happened so far." Quinn stared out the window. "I don't know if I can accept your offer."

"You've already done so. I have a contract proving it."

"I guaranteed a certificate of insurance as part of that agreement."

Geneva lowered her cup to its saucer. "I choose to ignore that clause."

One corner of Quinn's mouth quirked in one of his fleeting half grins. "Makes me a bit hesitant to continue working with someone who can choose to ignore the fine print on a contract when it pleases her."

Geneva relaxed back in her seat, enjoying their exchange in spite of the circumstances. "You should learn to take advantage of a weakness or an opportunity when it presents itself."

"Maybe I'm hesitant to do that, too," he said, "considering my history of being the party with the weaknesses and lost opportunities."

"Misplaced honor, Mr. Quinn?"

"Just Quinn. And yes, I misplaced my honor a long time ago."

They exchanged mild, understanding smiles as Missy brought their breakfasts. His troubles hadn't diminished his appetite, Geneva was relieved to notice.

"I've asked my investigator to speak with Reed Oberman," she said when Missy had left.

"What information does he have for the police?"

"Not much. But he does have a witness."

"To the vandalism?"

"To some suspicious activity." Geneva sipped her orange juice. "However, this witness isn't the most reliable source. It's the gentleman who spends so much of his time on the docks, fishing. Ed Morton."

"I know Ed. He may be a little strange, but I've never known him to rant or hallucinate." Quinn frowned. "Still, it doesn't help our case when the only witness so far is known to most people in the Cove as Crazy Ed."

"No, it doesn't. But I'm inclined to believe Ed, considering the way the information was obtained." Geneva glanced beyond Quinn's shoulder at the rest of the room, checking to make sure she wouldn't be overheard. "The investigator was very careful not to ask any leading questions. There wasn't much Ed could tell him, but he did say he's seen a blue truck near the site, late in the evening."

"How late?"

"After midnight."

"After midnight it's too dark to tell what color a truck is," Quinn pointed out.

"Ed said there's a very distinctive sticker on the rear fender." Geneva leaned forward. "Do you know of anyone who drives a blue pickup truck?"

"Yeah." Quinn's eyes narrowed. "I do."

"Does this person have any motive for sabotaging Tidewaters?"

"I thought so, at first, but now…" Quinn shook his head. "The spill doesn't fit. It doesn't help him, not the way he was looking for help. And he's not smart enough to figure out something like that on his own."

"Are you saying he might have been responsible for the first two incidents?"

"I've never considered the damage to the backhoe to be anything other than criminal mischief. Guess I should reconsider." He gave her a hard look. "But I've always had my own suspicions about how Ned got hurt."

"I'll arrange for you to meet with my investigator."

Geneva chatted pleasantly with Missy for a few minutes when the young woman returned to ask if their breakfasts were satisfactory, and she chose to maintain the same conversational tone when Missy had left. "How is your daughter?" she asked Quinn.

"Looking forward to the start of summer vacation." He forked up a piece of waffle. "Friday is the last day of school. I haven't figured out yet what to do with her. She keeps insisting she's old enough to stay by herself, and I know she's right, but not in this case."

"How old is she?"

"Ten."

"Ah, yes. I recall that age. Too old for a babysitter, but not old enough to be without supervision for an extended period of time." Geneva smiled. "Parenthood is never easy, particularly when it's done alone."

"My wife never complained," he said.

Geneva admired his attempt at fairness. "Your ex-wife," she clarified.

"Yes."

"I heard she's in Oregon."

"That's right."

"And yet Rosie is with you."

"It's my turn."

"To avoid complaining," Geneva said as she lifted her tea for another sip.

"I'm lucky to have my daughter with me," he said. "I intend to keep her."

"In spite of the fine print?"

He leveled a bland gaze across the table, and Geneva knew she'd stepped into dangerous territory. "We were discussing," she said, "the difficulties of keeping her supervised during the summer. Have you looked into any educational programs or camps?"

"No."

"Have you asked Tess for help?"

His gaze sharpened. "Why would I ask her?"

"Because she might know of something," Geneva said casually. "I understand she's recently spent some time in the Adams Elementary School office."

His face lit with amusement. "Yes, she has."

"She seems quite fond of your daughter."

The amusement faded. "I suppose so."

"Have you asked her?"

"We don't discuss Rosie."

"Perhaps you should," Geneva said. "My grand-daughter may surprise you, Quinn."

"She already has," he said with an unreadable expression.

"Good." Geneva lifted her napkin to her mouth. "I believe that's all I wanted to discuss with you today. If you'll excuse me…"

He rose as she exited the booth, and they exchanged polite goodbyes. She noticed, as she drove away, that he was still sitting in the booth, staring out the window.

The man had a great deal on his mind. Tess alone was enough to make any man sit and stare, pondering, for quite a long while.

CHAPTER EIGHTEEN

TESS GLANCED UP from her monitor when her little bell jangled shortly after lunch on Monday. Quinn strode toward her desk, dropped into one of her visitor's chairs and stared at her floor.

"How bad is it?" she asked.

"Bad enough. There's no way to know for sure."

"What are you going to do?"

"How do you feel about a water feature in front of the building?"

"What kind of water feature?"

"A small lake."

She swallowed, and she was sure she could actually feel her face pale beneath her carefully applied makeup. "That's not in the budget," she said.

"There is no budget." He raised his eyes to hers. "This project is now officially out of control. And you and I both know there are forces at work behind the scenes trying to make sure this thing never gets resolved satisfactorily."

"Cobb."

"Among others." Quinn shifted and settled more heavily in his chair. "He wasn't the only one contesting the environmental impact report's conclusions."

"I'll talk with Geneva and—"

"I've talked with her. I met with her this morning. For breakfast. And before you start giving me grief over that," he said, raising his hand, "you told me you don't do mornings."

She closed her file and rolled the mouse precisely to the center of its pad. "I would have made an exception in this case." Again.

"The thing is," he said in his irritatingly reasonable tone, "you've already been paid the lion's share of what you'll make on this project. The design is done, bought and paid for. I've got a payroll to meet and men who are wondering when the next one will be. Your design isn't the problem. Getting it built is mine."

"Isn't there some way to continue to work around the cleanup?" she asked.

"Not for a while. A week, maybe."

"What will you do?"

He stood and paced to one of her models and stared down at it, his hands in his pockets. The winery, the one he'd admired. He'd surprised her, not so long ago, with his concise, spot-on summary of the heart of her design.

He looked so big, looming over her model, so strong and sure. She often forgot how many people were counting on him, how many responsibilities he bore on a daily basis. "Don't you worry about me," he said. "I can always find work." He gave her a wry smile. "Men with tool belts are very popular."

She rose from her seat and went to him. "They're very attractive, too."

He cupped her face in his big, strong, sure hands. "Think so?"

"One of the main reasons I went into this line of work. For the view."

His gaze softly touched all her features. "We'll be okay, Tess. We'll find some way to work around this."

"All right."

"What?" He drew back. "No argument?"

She wrapped her fingers around his wrists. "Actually, I don't think much of your water-feature idea."

"Okay. I can compromise on that." He brushed a sweet kiss across her lips, paused and moved in for another. And then another, as the familiar heat simmered and snapped between them. He dropped his hands to her waist and yanked her close. *"Tess."*

"I'm here."

"Yes," he murmured against her throat. "You are."

She grabbed his collar and hung on tight while he carried them both away from their troubles for a few moments, and then she floated back to earth on a sigh. "I like what you can do to me, Quinn."

"Good. Because I plan on doing it a lot."

He shifted an inch away and took her by the chin. "I wasn't sure why I came here today or what I'd say when I walked through your door. But I'm glad I did."

"I'm glad, too," she said as he left.

She moved to her window and watched him shove two quarters into the meter near her car. And ordered herself not to fall in love with him.

QUINN STALKED into his office trailer on Saturday morning and threw a fistful of invoices on his counter. He'd been able to cling to his insurance so far, and he'd received permission to continue work on the building while the En-Tech engineers hauled away the contaminated soil. They'd been lucky; there was no sign yet of a leak into the bay.

He should be grateful he was still here, making progress, but sometimes the daily dose of insanity got to be too much. "Goddamn it," he muttered.

"Dad." Rosie swiveled in his chair, spinning in a clumsy circle. "You're not setting a very good example for the kid."

He grinned at her use of Tess's term, relieved the two women in his life had begun to reach some sort of understanding. The basis for that understanding made him a little nervous—and he was too cowardly to examine it too closely—but at least it was an improvement on that disastrous first dinner scene.

Enough of an improvement, perhaps, to try his luck with the next step. He may have been having more success recently managing his urges to take a drink, but his craving for a certain woman's company seemed beyond his control. "I'm thinking about taking Tess out for dinner."

Rosie halted her swiveling and frowned.

"Or not," Quinn said.

She tilted her head, and her frown tugged to one side. "I guess it's your turn."

"What do you mean?"

"She brought the food last time."

He leaned his elbows on the counter. "I'm thinking this dinner with Tess would be like…like a date."

"*Like* a date?"

"Okay. A date." His face was heating. "Which means you're not invited."

She shrugged. "That's cool."

"It is?"

"Yeah." She resumed her swiveling. "If you leave me with a pizza. And a new video. Maybe that one about the spaceship and the pirates."

"And Neva."

Rosie's skinny chest lifted and collapsed with a grown-up-size sigh. "Two videos, then."

"That's extortion."

"Is that like blackmail?"

Quinn muttered an oath under his breath as he gathered the invoices and tapped their edges into a neater stack. "Tess was right to wonder about the crap they're teaching you in school these days."

TESS STOOD outside Quinn's apartment door, waiting for the flutters in her stomach to quiet. She knew what was coming—a few scorching glances, some deliciously teasing verbal foreplay and then a frenzied, mindless, glorious bout of lovemaking. It would all leave her exhilarated and exhausted and struggling to resurrect clear boundaries between lust and longing.

Boundaries she was considering ahead of schedule.

This had to stop. She was a woman who knew how to handle an affair, a woman who knew how to keep things casual and make a smooth exit.

The trouble was she'd lost sight of the exit sign.

Her hand, when she raised it to knock on his door, was trembling. And her heart, when he opened his door and pulled her inside, seemed to stumble and stop.

It wasn't the soft jazz whispering from Rosie's purple player in the corner, or the tangled iris stalks stuffed inexpertly into a juice pitcher on the small table, or the candles burning beside them or the kiss he brushed over her knuckles that made her nerves bubble and her breath catch in a jerky sigh. It was the look in his eyes, the intense gaze that told her he had no doubts about this evening. No reasons to hide anything from her—his desire, his affection, his delight in what they would share.

And oh, she wanted that, too—that certainty that everything would work out in the end, that they could make love and remain friends. Surely that was the reason her face was so warm and her mouth was so dry.

"Can I get you a drink?" he asked.

"A drink? Yes. I— Yes. Water. Please."

She dropped her purse on the sofa and walked to the window, rubbing her hands over her arms. She thought she recognized the tune floating through the air, and bits of phrases flitted through her mind as she tried to piece together the lyrics. She focused on the words, trying to sort out the rest of the song. It was easier than trying to sort the sensations tangling and knotting inside her.

"Tess." Quinn's voice was a caress as he handed her the glass. He waited patiently as she sipped, and then he gently tugged the drink from her hand, placed it on the windowsill and slowly pulled her into a dancer's embrace.

"What are you doing?" she asked.

"Dancing with you." His fingers spread in a warm fan across the small of her back, urging her closer.

"Why?"

"Why not?" He rested his cheek against hers, so softly. So sweetly. "I've been wanting to hold you all week."

"You can do that later. In bed." Could he hear the panic in her voice?

"I've been wanting that, too. Waiting for that." He took her hand and curled her fingers in his, against his chest. "Imagining how it will be."

"Last time was pretty good." She reminded herself to wrap her arms around his neck, to press her body against his, to take the lead and get things moving. But they were already moving, and she couldn't seem to find her balance, couldn't take control.

"Have you been waiting?" he asked, ignoring her remark.

"Of course I have." She let out a sigh that sounded more shaky than disgusted. "Quinn, I—"

He pressed a soft, moist kiss to her temple. "Hmm?"

"I...um..." Whatever point she'd been about to make, the thought disappeared as his lips skimmed along her cheek. "What are you doing?"

"Kissing you."

"No, you're not."

He smiled as he guided her through an easy turn and then rested his forehead against hers. "I'm not?"

"No." She sighed as he touched his mouth to hers, once, twice, as light as a wish. "You're up to something."

"Maybe."

"Maybe?" She pulled away and stared at him, searching his face for some sign of the serious, cynical man she'd come to know so well. But he wasn't here tonight.

He took her hand, the one cupped in his, and flattened it against his chest. Beneath her palm, beneath his soft sweater, his heart beat steadily. So strong, so sure.

"I want tonight to be different," he said.

"Does this mean we're going to eat first?"

"If you'd like."

His beautiful mouth turned up at the edges, and his smile warmed her clear through and scared her to death. "I want to seduce you, Tess."

She swallowed. "That would explain the flowers and candles."

"Mere props." His hand brushed up her back, and his fingers stroked her nape, sending ice chips and sparks skittering up and down her spine. "I've got more than music and mood to offer tonight."

"I don't need those things. I'm here. I'm ready and willing. What more do you want?"

"More." He pulled her closer. "This. Everything we can do together. Be together."

"I already told you," she said in a voice gone breathless, "I'm willing to do whatever you want."

"Be mine." He stilled and lifted her fingers to his mouth to graze her knuckles with his lips. "For tonight. Let me make you feel as though it's forever."

Oh, no. *No.* Not this—not romance. She couldn't take it, couldn't handle it, not from him. Not from Quinn, of all people, and not now, not when she was trembling and weakening with every ridiculous dance step in this slightly shabby setting. "I don't—"

"Tess." He released her and cradled her face in his hands. "Kiss me, Tess."

And then she was kissing him and sliding into his steady, strong embrace, and letting go, just a little. Enjoying the moment, as much as she could. Part of her was still terrified of what he could do to her, of what he could make her feel, if she let him.

He spun the kiss out, tender and sweet, testing and savoring. Another tune began, something hinting of heartbreak with the sly purr of a throaty clarinet. On the street below, a passing car tooted its horn, and someone shouted a rough response. She curled her fingers into his sweater, holding on, holding tight. Trying to hold back, to keep a part of herself safe and secure.

The effort made her dizzy. That's what it was—it couldn't be a mere kiss that had left her so lightheaded.

"I think I need more water," she said when he inched back to stare at her. "I'm feeling a little…um…"

"Ready for more?"

"There's more?" she whispered.

He swept her into his arms and carried her down the hall. "Don't expect this kind of a ride every time," he said, his eyes crinkling at the corners. "I know you like variety."

"Variety?"

He gently lowered her to his bed and showed her exactly what he meant, loving her as she'd never been loved before, with his heart in his touch and his soul in his gaze. And she gave herself up to him, loving him in return.

CHAPTER NINETEEN

QUINN CLIMBED into his truck well after midnight on Wednesday, bone-tired and brain-dead. Why was it that paperwork could wear a man down like nothing else?

He'd hoped to get back home sooner than this. Tess and Rosie were both there, having themselves a "girls' night," whatever the hell that was. He suspected the two of them were scheming, and he was unsure about what he'd find when he arrived.

He rubbed a hand across the back of his neck, digging his fingers into his nape and wondering if he could convince Tess to give him a quick massage before she left. If she did, he'd probably pass out, snoring, before she walked out the door—not the kind of impression he'd want to leave her with.

He yawned and shook his head, and then he pulled through the gate and left the motor running while he jogged back to close and lock the fencing. Strips of night fog swirled around the streetlamps, gliding on traces of the day's lingering warmth, and a couple of cats faced off in a yowling duet somewhere near the marina. No cars passed the waterfront, no lights glowed in the black windows up and down the street or on the boats moored at the docks. Except for Quinn and the cats, everyone in this part of town had turned in hours ago.

He returned to his seat and pulled his car phone from the glove box. He'd call Tess to tell her he was on his way back and try to keep her chatting. His personal talk radio. "Hey, Tess," he said when she answered.

"Where are you?"

"Headed home."

"At last," she said.

He could hear the television in the background, something with a hyperactive rock beat and sarcastic commentary. "Rosie still awake?"

"Hope that's not a problem." Tess must have placed her hand over the phone, because her next words were muffled. The television volume decreased a few degrees. "She wanted to wait up for you."

"No problem." His truck idled at an intersection, waiting for the signal to change. "How did things go?"

"Fine. We made popcorn and did our nails and talked about boys."

"Boys?"

"You'd prefer it if we talked about men?"

"No." He grinned as he pulled through the intersection. "I was wondering what you contributed to the discussion."

"Hey. I used to date boys."

"So you provided the expertise."

"On boys? No way. I don't know the guys in Rosie's class."

Neither did he, Quinn realized. He was suddenly much less sleepy.

"By the way," Tess said, "you're out of milk."

"We had half a carton when I left."

"Sorry. Hot cocoa to wash down the popcorn."

Quinn tugged on the wheel and angled around another corner, heading back in the direction he'd come from.

"Guess I'll pick some up at the twenty-four-hour place near the marina on the way there. See you in ten minutes."

"Okay. Quinn?"

"Yeah?"

"Your kid's okay."

He tossed the phone on the paperwork spread on the bench seat beside him, his grin spreading so wide he thought his face would crack. A guy had to fall for a woman who was a sucker for his kid.

Happiness and hope were rusty things, snagging on the tight spots as they struggled up from somewhere deep inside him, scrambling toward the surface. Damn, it felt good. Light and tingly and nearly as heady as one of Tess's kisses. He'd been afraid to set those feelings loose, to let them spread and settle, but things between him and Tess and Rosie had been going so well lately that it—

He coasted to the curb a couple of blocks from Tidewaters and switched off the ignition. Sinking low in his seat, he waited, nerves taut, for the automatic light to dim and give him another glimpse of what he thought he'd seen. There it was, on the second level, deep within the shadowy angles of Tidewaters' hulking silhouette. A momentary streak of faint light.

A flashlight's beam.

He opened his door, slid from the seat to the pavement and carefully closed the truck, holding his breath as the latch caught with a quiet snick. He paused again, crouched beside the black door, grateful for his dark clothing, waiting for another sign the intruder was still there. Again, that faint sweep of light, farther to the north.

The bastard wouldn't get away with whatever he had planned for tonight.

Quinn darted across the street and down the block,

keeping to the shadows beneath the trees dotting the sidewalk, avoiding the fog-misted spotlights below the streetlamps. Stealthily, scanning the construction site every few yards, he moved to the gate, and then he silently swore as he fumbled with the lock in the darkness. He'd forgotten his cell phone in his truck. He couldn't be sure he'd have time to cut across the site to reach the phone in his trailer, and the squawk of the metal door might give him away.

The combination lock sprang open, and Quinn slipped inside and caught the gate with the latch, leaving it unlocked. He had to move across open space now, in clear view of whoever was up there. He slowly stood, his senses straining, his heart pounding and his breath coming in short puffs. Again, the light, shifting along the north side, and then disappearing.

He focused on the ground and ran a jagged path, skirting the edge of En-Tech's massive dig. He aimed for the smooth spots where the gravel had settled into the mud, where he'd have less chance of crunching over loose rocks or catching a stone with his boot toe and sending it clanging against a piece of equipment. A dense layer of fog blotted the moonlight as he passed through one of the gaping doorways on the east side of the structure. He ducked behind a stack of siding and paused again, listening for some sound, some sign of discovery or a hint of what the intruder was doing here.

He waited, too, until his breath came in slower, deeper gasps, and it was then that he smelled it. Gasoline. The pungent stench was overpowering.

God. He was going to burn the place down.

Quinn sprinted from his crouch and pounded up the stairs, dashing around partial walls and leaping over piles of material. He slipped on the powdery residue of sawdust and nearly fell against the air compressor, the humid night air clogging his lungs and his pulse throbbing in his ears as he raced toward the place he'd last seen the light. No one there. "I know you're here," he shouted. "I've called the cops."

Silence.

Quinn slid through a stud wall, edging toward the open ramp leading to the third floor, his thoughts racing. No plywood cladding on the walls up there, no railing in too many places on that level. He didn't want to climb up and risk a confrontation and a fall. But the stink of oil hung thick in the mist around him here. He had to get out, to get to the scaffolding or—

He ducked and swung, low, toward the scuffling sound of a footstep behind him, raising an arm to protect his head. Something glanced off his arm, sloshing liquid to blind him and soak his hair before smashing to the floor. Glass shards crunched beneath his boots as he plowed into the figure, taking them both down, hard, on the thick plywood. Shocking pain shot through his jaw, and another blow landed on his head as the intruder grunted and squirmed, a mass of flailing arms and legs. They rolled once, twice, before the intruder shoved and kicked free, catching Quinn in the ribs and punching the breath out of him.

He lurched upright, tangling and tripping in the compressor hose as he staggered toward the black gap in the floor where steps led to the ground level. A moment later a muffled *whoomph* echoed through the structure, and flames licked up the stair opening to spread in oily waves along the floor, flowing toward his feet.

He dove for an opening in the plywood wall and

dropped to the ground two levels below. He landed crookedly, an ankle twisting beneath him. Rolling to his back, his breath burst from his throat in a strangled grunt and he stared up at Tidewaters, glowing orange and gold, cloaked in roiling black smoke. The air crackled and stank of fuel and burning pitch. *"No."*

The sound of an engine whined over the roar of the fire. Quinn struggled to his feet and stumbled toward the headlight beams shining on the trailer. He detoured to the chop saw raised on its temporary sawhorse, grabbed a crowbar and swung as the dark truck moved past him. The windshield cracked and the bar caught in its frame. The driver swerved, dragging Quinn through the gravel and mud before the truck's tires skidded and spun, seeking purchase along the sharp edge of the spill excavation. The chassis shuddered and tilted over the yawning gap, and Quinn's legs swung over nothingness as he lost his grip on the bar.

He tumbled into the hole and rolled, digging and clawing and scrambling away from the edge, out from beneath the pickup he was sure would roll onto its side and crush him. But in the next breath he heard the thud and ping of rocks pelting the depression around him, and he curled into a tight ball, covering his head to protect it from the rear tire as it gained traction. Pea gravel stung his back like wasps.

He hauled himself to his knees to peer beyond the rim of the excavation, watching as the truck crashed through the gate, one fence section collapsing and catching on its hood to trawl behind, out into the street. And then the stiff wire section clattered to the pavement as the truck picked up speed and disappeared into the siren-screaming distance.

"WHEN DID Dad say he was coming home?" Rosie switched channels again, and Tess snatched the remote from her hand.

"Ten minutes."

"Ten minutes was up ten minutes ago. It's tomorrow already. He missed our party."

"That's what we get for planning a surprise party. The surprise is on us." Tess tried to shrug off the trickle of anxiety, but she glanced toward the window. "He'll be here."

"I'm tired." Rosie yawned and flipped over, stretching out on her stomach. "Call him again."

"He'll think I'm nagging."

"He's used to it."

"I don't nag."

"Ha."

Tess muttered something uncomplimentary about the kid as she dug through her purse for her phone. She punched in Quinn's number, waited through the ring tones and got his voice mail. "He's not answering."

"He always answers." Rosie shifted upright. "Something's wrong."

"Maybe the batteries ran low. Maybe he left it in his car when he went into the store," she said, although she knew he wouldn't do that. He always had a phone with him. He wanted to stay in touch with his daughter. "Maybe—"

Sirens squealed to life, nerve-racking and earsplitting and so close Tess jumped from the sofa. "What's that?"

"The fire department." Rosie stumbled to the window and stared down at the street. "It's right around the corner."

"No kidding." Tess rubbed her arms. "How do you sleep through that?"

"We don't." Rosie turned, her face streaked and dotted with the ghastly glow of neon strobes. "What if that's for Dad?"

"It's not."

"What if it is?" Rosie ran to her room. "I'm getting my coat," she called over her shoulder.

"Good idea." Tess flinched as another screaming vehicle roared down the street below the apartment window. She grabbed her jacket. "Let's go."

She locked the door behind Rosie, and they raced together down the hall.

TESS TRAILED the wailing sirens through the heart of town, breaking several traffic laws as she drove her roadster toward the hellfire coiling red and black above the bay fog. Oh God oh God oh God. Tidewaters. *Quinn.*

Her car shot through the gaping hole where the gate had been and spun to a stop beside a fire engine. She crawled out, grabbed Rosie's hand and barreled through a knot of emergency crew, legs pumping, heart pounding, breath burning in her tight throat.

"Let me through," she yelled when one of the firefighters made a grab to stop her. Another stepped into her path, and she let go of Rosie's hand to try to shove past him. He grabbed her by the waist. "Let me go."

"Wait a minute, lady." Another firefighter nabbed Rosie by her coat sleeve. "You can't go up there."

"My dad's up there," Rosie said.

"No one's up there."

"Are you sure?" Tess sagged in the firefighter's arms. "How can you be sure?"

"Crawford." A man in a different uniform stepped forward. "Take these women to the trailer."

The firefighter named Crawford gripped Tess's arm and Rosie's and escorted them to the trailer. Along one of its corrugated metal sides, visible in the pulsing neon of the emergency vehicles, Tess saw huge lettering in an ugly, spray-painted scrawl—the acronym of a terrorist organization.

Environmental terrorists.

"No civilians past this point." A police officer stepped from the shadows near the trailer's door and met them at a bobbing line of yellow crime-scene ribbon. "Take these women back out to the street."

"This is Quinn's daughter," Tess said, yanking her arm free of Crawford's grip.

"And who are you?" the officer asked.

Tess opened her mouth to reply and froze. The project architect. Quinn's lover. A friend. None of the phrases seemed to have enough power to get her past the barrier and through that door to be by Quinn's side, to see for herself if he was all right.

"She's my dad's fiancée," Rosie told the men.

Crawford raised the yellow crime-scene tape. "Let them through."

Tess followed Rosie toward the short metal steps. "Why did you tell them I'm his fiancée?"

"I saw it in a movie." She shot Tess a bland glance over her shoulder. "It worked, didn't it?"

"This is real life, kid," Tess said as she shoved the trailer door open. "No happy endings here."

Inside, two men in uniform stood at the counter, and beyond them, in his desk chair, sat Quinn.

"Dad!"

Rosie dashed around the corner and threw herself into his arms. He scooped her up and into his lap, burying his face in her hair for a long moment before looking up, across the room, to where Tess stood.

She took a step forward and then stopped, staring at him, at his sticky hair and bloodshot eyes, at his torn and muddied clothing. And she breathed in the smell of him, the sickly sweet smell of whiskey that permeated the air around him.

"You're okay," she said.

"Yeah."

"Good," she managed.

And then, her heart numb and her brain buzzing, she crumpled and crept into the safety of a familiar, black nothingness deep inside, and she turned and walked out the door.

CHAPTER TWENTY

QUINN SAGGED against the unforgiving back of the wooden visitor's chair in Reed Oberman's corner of the police station late Thursday morning, feeling every bruise he'd acquired the night before. He'd taken Rosie home and tucked her into bed, showered and collapsed on his own mattress. And then he'd lain awake, staring at his ceiling, reliving the night's events. Reliving the surging rage and the heart-stopping terror and the knee-buckling pain, until the evening shadows faded to filmy daylight.

Hunger and thirst had driven him from bed shortly after seven, and he'd limped through the front room, heading toward the kitchen, hoping a bowl of cereal and a glass of juice would cure the insomnia that exhaustion hadn't been able to dent. It was then that he'd discovered what Tess had done, what he hadn't noticed a few hours earlier when he'd carried a sleeping Rosie down the hall.

His front room had been painted a soft, silvery green. Plump new pillows on his old brown sofa picked up the beautiful color in lively tones, and a watercolor print of a lighthouse on a sandy shore hung on the wall above. She'd managed to make his run-down, secondhand space seem updated and inviting without changing much of anything at all.

Imagine what she might have done with me, he'd thought, if she'd cared enough to stick around and try.

He'd stared at the walls and the print, at the pretty bakery cake and festive party things arranged on his coffee table. And then he'd closed his eyes and seen again the revulsion in her face when she'd come close enough to smell Wade's whiskey on his clothes, and he'd heard again her flat, emotionless voice when she'd turned her back on him.

Damn. Needing Tess more than he'd ever needed a drink was a hell of an improvement in his addictions. He'd stood there, in that room she'd brightened, fighting the pressure building in his chest and the thick, hot pain clogging his throat. And then he'd returned to his room to dress.

After leaving Neva to watch over his still-sleeping daughter, he'd come to the police station to make another statement and check on the status of the investigation. He had to do something, make some sort of progress. Like a shark, if he stopped moving, he'd drown.

Reed returned to his cubicle and dropped heavily into his desk chair. He rubbed a hand over his reddened eyes and sighed. "Wade isn't changing his story. He's still insisting he acted alone."

"Did you offer him a deal?"

"Working on it." Reed tipped back in his creaky chair and yawned. "Still trying to convince the DA there's enough evidence to point to an accessory."

"There isn't any evidence."

"There's the problem." Reed frowned. "It's not that I don't believe you, it's just that—"

"It's easier to hang this on Wade and forget about the conspiracy angle."

Reed nodded. "We've got a witness, we've got a truck showing damage consistent with reported events, we've got forensic evidence in that same truck and on

Wade's clothes. And we've got a confession. It's an open-and-shut case."

"Neat and tidy." Quinn shifted in his chair, his own words a fresh reminder of the pain this had caused Tess, as he forced down another surge of anger. "Except for what was spray-painted on the side of my trailer."

"Wade's confessed to that, too."

"Did you ask him what it meant?"

Reed glanced up. "No."

"Ask him. If he knows what it means, ask him how he heard about it, where he got the idea in the first place. Press him for the details." Quinn stood, wincing as he straightened. "You and I both know Wade's too stupid to plan things through like this. He had a fairly strong motive for cutting that board on the scaffolding. He didn't have any reason to cause that spill or start that fire. He came looking for a job—he wouldn't have wanted to destroy the job site that might have given it to him."

"There's one motive you haven't mentioned," Reed said. "Revenge."

Quinn stopped in the doorway and glanced over his shoulder. "It's a sorry testament to my life to admit I can consider that as another possibility."

TESS KICKED OFF her shoes and stretched out on the plush sofa in her grandmother's blue parlor the evening after the fire. They'd shared a quiet dinner in the kitchen, allowing Julia to cluck and fuss over them both and soothe them with asparagus bisque and steaming sour-dough baguettes fresh from the oven. The thought of returning alone to her house, of waking in her empty bed and beginning again in the morning was overwhelming. "I'm too tired to move, Mémère. Maybe I'll stay right in this spot for the rest of the week."

"Nonsense. We've more to do—and more reasons to do it—than ever." Geneva poured herself a cup of tea. "Although I must admit this project has turned out to be more of a challenge than I'd expected."

Tess laughed sourly. "Your talent for understatement never ceases to amaze me."

"And your capacity for passion has never failed to disappoint me." Geneva continued. "So why do I get the feeling you're not as angry over what has happened or as determined to see this through as I thought you'd be?"

"I don't know. It's the shock, I suppose." Tess rolled her head more comfortably against a pillow and closed her eyes. "I'm just so tired."

"I've heard depression can sap one's energy."

"I'm not depressed. I just— I haven't had much sleep lately."

The clock on the mantel chimed its deep, metallic bong, marking another hour of her life. Tess had always loved that sound, but tonight it seemed…

Depressing.

She shifted on her side and studied her grandmother. "Did you love Grandpa, Mémère? Always? Even toward the end, when he was so sick?"

"Not in the same way. He wasn't the same man at that point." Geneva sighed and smoothed a hand over the soft throw on her lap. "And anything I may tell you about my relationship with your grandfather has nothing at all to do with you and Quinn. You're two different people."

"He's an alcoholic, Mémère." Tess rolled to her back and stared at the beamed and plastered ceiling. "I swore I'd never get involved with a man who had that problem."

"*Had* is a word in the past tense. And it's another convenient excuse."

"Why are all excuses convenient?" Tess's eyelids

drifted shut. "Why can't they be excellent, or justified, or brilliant?"

"I suppose I should sit quietly and be supportive," Geneva said impatiently, "or serve as a sounding board while you work your way through your quandary. But I've never enjoyed that particular role in any relationship."

"This isn't just a relationship," Tess said. "I'm your granddaughter."

"And that's why I've tolerated your foolishness for as long as I have this evening."

Tess sat upright and faced her grandmother. "I'm trying not to be foolish. I'm trying to consider everything that could possibly go wrong."

"And looking for reasons—or excuses—to back out of the first serious love affair you've had for years."

"Maybe that's what I want to do, deep down inside." Tess stared at the clock, unable to face her grandmother's stern gaze. "Back out of this."

"Would that make you happy?"

"No. Not now. But maybe, in the future, I'll be glad I took some time to think about this."

"You've had several months to think about this," Geneva said as she lifted the cup to her lips.

"I haven't been thinking about marriage."

"No. But you've been thinking about the man." She paused for a sip. "What do you think of him, Tess?"

"What do *you* think of him, Mémère? And please, don't tell me it's none of my business. Or that this is none of yours. I want to know. Why did you hire him to do this job?"

"Because I believed he'd be strong enough to stand up to you." She set the tea aside. "And because on the surface, he appeared to be exactly the wrong man for you, so I didn't worry you'd be suspicious about my real motives."

"What do you mean, your real motives?"

"I may be an old lady, Tess dear, but I'm not blind. Quinn is a handsome, virile man. A caring father who values family, from what I've observed."

"Mémère." Tess fell back against the cushions, shocked to her core. "You hired a stud for your own granddaughter."

"I'm glad you agree about the stud factor. I told you, I have a great deal of experience reading people. Close your mouth, Tess dear. It's unattractive to let your jaw hang open like that." Geneva flapped a hand in Tess's direction. "As you told me yourself, I can be one hell of a scary lady."

"Then I'm sure you'll get the results you want," Tess told her steely spined grandmother with a grin. "You always do, Mémère."

QUINN SAT on his sofa that night, cushioned by pretty pillows, his daughter tucked beside him.

"Dad. Talk to me." Rosie pulled the remote from his hand and switched off the television. "You can say anything. You can't say anything worse than stuff I've already said to myself, a dozen times."

"That sounds familiar."

She shrugged. "I probably heard it on TV. On one of those sappy family shows. The ones with the perfect parents and the perfect kids."

"No one would watch a show like that."

"Don't change the subject."

"That sounds familiar, too," he said. She pinched him, hard. *"Ow,"* he said, rubbing his arm.

"You're upset about Tess, right?"

"Yeah," he admitted. "How'd you know?"

"Lately, everything is about Tess."

"That's not right," he said, frowning. "Everything is supposed to be about you."

Rosie shifted away with a disgusted snort. "No wonder you're having problems."

They sat in silence for a while, and then she began to twist the ring Tess had bought for her on one of their afternoon shopping trips. "Maybe this *is* about me," she said. "About me and Tess. And you and Tess. About the three of us."

"The three of us?"

Twist, twist, twist. "Do you love her?"

"Yeah," he said with an unhappy sigh. "I do."

"Does she love you?"

"I don't know. I mean, I don't know why she would, but—yeah." He shrugged away the hurt. "I'm pretty sure she does."

"Dad." Rosie shifted to face him. "This is awesome."

"It is?"

"Of course it is. Now you can marry her, and we can go live in her house, and I can get a dog, and she can pick me up every day from school and—"

"I haven't asked her to marry me yet."

"Well, are you going to?"

"I don't know."

"Dad."

"Rosie." He rubbed a hand over his eyes, fuzzy with exhaustion and humming with nerves. "This is important. I can't just ask someone to marry me so we can live at her house and get a dog."

"So ask her because you love her."

It sounded like a good idea, but maybe sleep deprivation and stress were twisting his thought processes like warm taffy. Tess might turn him down, but what did he have to lose by asking, except a chance to be with her forever?

Tess. Being with Tess forever was worth just about anything he'd have to do to get her to say yes.

"What about you?" he asked his daughter.

"Don't worry. I love her, too, Dad."

God, he was getting tired of this tendency toward hot, dry lumps in his throat. Unable to speak, he lifted his arm and dropped it around Rosie's shoulders to pull her closer.

"Dad." Her voice was muffled against his shirt.

"Yeah."

"Let go. You're acting like one of those sappy dads on TV."

He gave her one last squeeze before releasing her. "Don't worry," he said. "I don't think we're ever going to be one of those sappy families."

"Not while Tess is around." Rosie gave him what looked suspiciously like a sappy grin. "She won't let us."

QUINN STOOD outside Tess's office the next day, a bouquet of long-stemmed blue flowers in one hand and a cup of syrupy coffee in the other. He wished he had a ring, but he wanted to get the proposal out of the way first. Besides, Tess would be so picky about what he put on her finger he was safer letting her choose it.

The lady had great taste. Whatever she selected would likely bite a pretty big chunk out of his savings, but he had no doubt it would be the prettiest ring in the shop. He'd enjoy seeing it sparkle on her long, slender hand when she pointed to something on her computer monitor or clacked the keys on her keyboard or gestured as she told a tale. He'd like knowing it was on her hand when she walked down Main Street as if she owned the strip, with all the men watching and admiring and knowing she belonged to him.

And to Rosie.

Tess opened her door and stood with one hand on the knob and the other at her waist. "Are you going to stand out there all day?"

"No."

"Are you going to come in?"

"Yeah."

She turned and headed toward the back of the room. "You brought me coffee?" she asked over her shoulder.

"And flowers." He extended his arm. "Here."

"'Here.'" She took them from him and set them on her desk. "How romantic."

"You want romantic?"

"You tell me. Do I?"

He grew very still and stared at her, watching for some clue as to what he should say or do next.

She sucked in a deep breath and covered her eyes with her hands. "I'm sorry. I shouldn't snap at you. This time, anyway." She dropped her hands with a sigh. "And the flowers are very nice. Thank you."

"You'll need to put them in water." Quinn gestured awkwardly toward the bouquet and then let his arm drop. "Or something."

"I know what to do with flowers."

"I don't want to talk about the damn flowers."

"Fine." She set her hip against her desk and crossed her arms. "What *do* you want to talk about?"

"Howard Cobb, for a start."

She gripped the desk's edges until her knuckles turned white. "Has he been arrested?"

"Brought in for questioning. Wade couldn't keep his story straight for long, especially when parts of it never made much sense. He's a weak man. A coward. He'd need someone like Cobb to spur him on while giving him the idea for a cover.

"And Cobb had plenty of motive, not to mention a public record of fighting Geneva over the environmental angle. So." Tess dragged in a deep breath and exhaled a long sigh. "I guess this is the beginning of the end."

The end. Quinn's nerves hit hard, ahead of schedule. "So to speak."

An uncomfortable silence filled the space between them. Neither of them moved. Eventually, Tess picked up the coffee he'd brought her and sipped.

"Sweet enough?" he asked.

"Perfect. Thanks." She sipped again, staring at him over the rim of the cup. "Is there something else you want to talk about?" she asked.

"Rosie."

"How's she doing?"

"Fine." He opened his mouth to say something else, one of the points he'd planned on making, but his spit had dried up along with his train of thought. "You like her, right?"

"She's okay, for a kid. A kid with a smart mouth and a lot of problems."

They're not my problems. I'm not the one who has to live with her.

"She's…" He cleared his throat. "She thinks…"

The alarms went off, and Tess swore as she circled her desk and grabbed her purse. "Damn meter. I swear, I—"

"Here." Quinn pulled a jar from his pocket and set it on her desk. "I brought you this, too."

Tess froze, her gaze locked on the fat condiment jar tied with a crumpled red bow and filled with quarters.

"Rosie added the ribbon," Quinn said to fill another strained silence. "She said it would look better that way. Sorry I smashed it." He poked at one of the loops, trying to make it right. "It looked a lot better when I left home."

"It's beautiful."

Tess's voice sounded funny, and Quinn glanced at her beautiful face. Suddenly it didn't look quite so attractive. It went all pale and sort of folded up like a slow-motion implosion, and her nose was turning an ugly shade of red. And then her eyes brimmed with tears, and one of them plopped on her shiny black jacket and made an ugly splotch. "I'm sorry," he said.

"For what?" she asked.

"I don't know."

"Men," she said as she snatched a tissue from her fancy tissue holder. "What am I going to do with you?"

"You could marry me."

She blew her nose with a snorty, wet, honking sound.

"Is that a yes?" he asked.

"No!"

"Oh. Well." He glanced at the jar of quarters and gestured awkwardly toward them. "You can keep the change."

"Quinn."

"Yeah?"

She sucked in a deep breath and blew it out again. "You're supposed to tell me you love me."

"Telling me how to do my job again?"

"Someone has to."

"All right." He took her hand, raised it to his lips and brushed them over her knuckles. "I love you, Tess."

"A kiss would be nice."

He lifted her hand higher. "I just gave you one."

"On the lips, Quinn."

He stared at her red nose and puffy eyes and closed his own eyes, tightly, before pressing a short, sweet kiss to her mouth. "There."

"'There.' Such a way with words."

He narrowed his eyes. "I don't hear any coming from you."

She moved in close, snugging her curvy front up against his and wrapping her arms around his neck and tangling her fingers in his hair, just the way he liked it. "I love you, J. J. Quinn. With all my heart. And I love your little girl, too. And yes, I'll marry you. And I'll— *Damn.*"

She shoved him aside and dashed out her door, yelling at the officer tucking a parking ticket beneath her car's wiper blade.

He shoved his hands into his pockets and strolled to the window—his heart as light as his step—to watch Tess rip the ticket from her car, crumple it in her manicured hands, toss it to the pavement and grind it beneath her spiky high heel.

A guy had to love a woman like that.

* * * * *

Don't miss the next BUILT TO LAST *romance from award-winning author Terry McLaughlin! Coming in December 2009.*

Celebrate 60 years of pure
reading pleasure with Harlequin®!

Harlequin Presents® is proud to introduce
its gripping new miniseries,
THE ROYAL HOUSE OF KAREDES.
An exquisite coronation diamond,
split as a symbol of a warring royal family's feud,
is missing! But whoever reunites the
diamond halves will rule all....

Welcome to eight brand-new titles that
unfold to reveal the stories of kings and queens,
princes and princesses torn apart by pride and
power, but finally reunited by love.

Step into the world of Karedes with
BILLIONAIRE PRINCE, PREGNANT MISTRESS
Available July 2009
from Harlequin Presents®.

ALEXANDROS KAREDES, SNOW DUSTING the shoulders of his leather jacket and glittering like jewels in his dark hair, stood at the door. Maria felt the blood drain from her head.

"Good evening, Ms. Santos."

His voice was as she remembered it. Deep. Husky. Perfect English, but with the faintest hint of a Greek accent. And cold, as cold as it had been that awful morning she would never forget, when he'd accused her of horrible things, called her terrible names....

"Aren't you going to ask me in?"

She fought for composure. Last time they'd faced each other, they'd been on his turf. Now they were on hers. She was in command here, and that meant everything.

"There's a sign on the door downstairs," she said, her tone every bit as frigid as his. "It says, 'No soliciting or vagrants.'"

His lips drew back in a wolfish grin. "Very amusing."

"What do you want, Prince Alexandros?"

A tight smile eased across his mouth and it killed her that even now, knowing he was a vicious, arrogant man, she couldn't help but notice what a handsome mouth it was. Chiseled. Generous. Beautiful, like the rest of him, which made him living proof that beauty could, indeed, be only skin deep.

"Such formality, Maria. You were hardly so proper the last time we were together."

She knew his choice of words was deliberate. She felt her face heat; she couldn't help that but she damned well didn't have to let him lure her into a verbal sparring match.

"I'll ask you once more, your highness. What do you want?"

"Ask me in and I'll tell you."

"I have no intention of asking you in. Tell me why you're here or don't. It's your choice, just as it will be my choice to shut the door in your face."

He laughed. It infuriated her, but she could hardly blame him. He was tall—six two, six three—and though he stood with one shoulder leaning against the door frame, hands tucked casually into the pockets of the jacket, his pose was deceptive. He was strong, with the leanly muscled body of a well-trained athlete.

She remembered his body with painful clarity. The feel of him under her hands. The power of him moving over her. The taste of him on her tongue.

Suddenly, he straightened, his laughter gone. "I have not come this distance to stand in your doorway," he said coldly, "and I am not going to leave until I am ready to do so. I suggest you stand aside and stop behaving like a petulant child."

A petulant child? Was that what he thought? This man who had spent hours making love to her and had then accused her of—of trading her body for profit?

Except it had not been love, it had been sex. And the sooner she got rid of him, the better.

She let go of the doorknob and stepped aside. "You have five minutes."

He strolled past her, bringing cold air and the scent of the night with him. She swung toward him, arms folded. He reached past her, pushed the door closed, then folded his arms, too. She wanted to open the door again but she'd be damned if she was going to get into a who's-in-charge-here argument with him. She was in charge, and he would surely see a tussle over the ground rules as a sign of weakness.

Instead, she looked past him at the big clock above her work table.

"Ten seconds gone," she said briskly. "You're wasting time, your highness."

"What I have to say will take longer than five minutes."

"Then you'll just have to learn to economize. More than five minutes, I'll call the police."

Instantly, his hand was wrapped around her wrist. He tugged her toward him, his dark chocolate eyes almost black with anger.

"You do that and I'll tell every tabloid shark I can contact about how Maria Santos tried to buy a five-hundred-thousand-dollar commission by seducing a prince." He smiled thinly. "They'll lap it up."

* * * * *

*What will it take for this billionaire prince to
realize he's falling in love with his mistress…?
Look for*
BILLIONAIRE PRINCE, PREGNANT MISTRESS
*by Sandra Marton
Available July 2009
from Harlequin Presents®.*

We'll be spotlighting a different series every month
throughout 2009 to celebrate our 60th anniversary.

Look for Harlequin® Presents in July!

TWO CROWNS, TWO ISLANDS, ONE LEGACY
A royal family, torn apart by pride and its lust for
power, reunited by purity and passion

Step into the world of Karedes
beginning this July with

BILLIONAIRE PRINCE,
PREGNANT MISTRESS
by
Sandra Marton

Eight volumes to collect and treasure!

HPBPA09

REQUEST YOUR FREE BOOKS!

2 FREE NOVELS PLUS 2 FREE GIFTS!

HARLEQUIN®

Super Romance®

Exciting, emotional, unexpected!

YES! Please send me 2 FREE Harlequin® Superromance® novels and my 2 FREE gifts (gifts are worth about $10). After receiving them, if I don't wish to receive any more books, I can return the shipping statement marked "cancel." If I don't cancel, I will receive 6 brand-new novels every month and be billed just $4.69 per book in the U.S. or $5.24 per book in Canada. That's a savings of close to 15% off the cover price! It's quite a bargain! Shipping and handling is just 50¢ per book*. I understand that accepting the 2 free books and gifts places me under no obligation to buy anything. I can always return a shipment and cancel at any time. Even if I never buy another book from Harlequin, the two free books and gifts are mine to keep forever.

135 HDN EYLG   336 HDN EYLS

Name	(PLEASE PRINT)	
Address		Apt. #
City	State/Prov.	Zip/Postal Code

Signature (if under 18, a parent or guardian must sign)

Mail to the **Harlequin Reader Service:**
IN U.S.A.: P.O. Box 1867, Buffalo, NY 14240-1867
IN CANADA: P.O. Box 609, Fort Erie, Ontario L2A 5X3

Not valid to current subscribers of Harlequin Superromance books.

**Are you a current subscriber of Harlequin Superromance books
and want to receive the larger-print edition?
Call 1-800-873-8635 today!**

* Terms and prices subject to change without notice. Prices do not include applicable taxes. Sales tax applicable in N.Y. Canadian residents will be charged applicable provincial taxes and GST. Offer not valid in Quebec. This offer is limited to one order per household. All orders subject to approval. Credit or debit balances in a customer's account(s) may be offset by any other outstanding balance owed by or to the customer. Please allow 4 to 6 weeks for delivery. Offer available while quantities last.

Your Privacy: Harlequin is committed to protecting your privacy. Our Privacy Policy is available online at www.eHarlequin.com or upon request from the Reader Service. From time to time we make our lists of customers available to reputable third parties who may have a product or service of interest to you. If you would prefer we not share your name and address, please check here. ☐

HSR09R

From *New York Times* bestselling authors

CARLA NEGGERS

SUSAN MALLERY
KAREN HARPER

More Than Words:
STORIES OF STRENGTH

They're your neighbors, your aunts, your sisters and your best friends. They're women across North America committed to changing and enriching lives, one good deed at a time. Three of these exceptional women have been selected as recipients of Harlequin's More Than Words award. And three *New York Times* bestselling authors have kindly offered their creativity to write original short stories inspired by these real-life heroines.

Visit **www.HarlequinMoreThanWords.com**
to find out more, or to nominate
a real-life heroine in your life.

Proceeds from the sale of this book will be reinvested in Harlequin's charitable initiatives.

Available in March 2009 wherever books are sold.

SUPPORTING CAUSES OF CONCERN TO WOMEN HARLEQUIN
WWW.HARLEQUINMORETHANWORDS.COM

PHMTW668

INTRODUCING THE FIFTH ANNUAL
MORE THAN WORDS ANTHOLOGY

Five bestselling authors
Five real-life heroines

A little comfort, caring and compassion go a long way toward making the world a better place. Just ask the dedicated women handpicked from countless worthy nominees across North America to become this year's recipients of Harlequin's More Than Words award. To celebrate their accomplishments, five bestselling authors have honored the winners by writing short stories inspired by these real-life heroines.

New stories inspired by real women who've changed lives

HEATHER GRAHAM

NEW YORK TIMES BESTSELLING AUTHOR

More Than Words
VOLUME 5

CANDACE CAMP
STEPHANIE BOND
BRENDA JACKSON
TARA TAYLOR QUINN

Visit **www.HarlequinMoreThanWords.com**
to find out more, or to nominate
a real-life heroine in your life.

**Proceeds from the sale of this book will be
reinvested in Harlequin's charitable initiatives.**

Available in April 2009 wherever books are sold.

THE BELLES OF TEXAS

They're as strong as the state that raised them. The Belle sisters aren't afraid to go after what they want, whether it's reclaiming their ranch or their family.

Linda Warren
CAITLYN'S PRIZE

Thanks to her deceased father's gambling debts, Caitlyn Belle's beloved High Five Ranch is in dire straits. Particularly because the will stipulates that if the ranch doesn't turn a profit in six months, it must be sold to Judd Calhoun—the man Caitlyn jilted fourteen years ago. And Cait knows Judd has been waiting a long time for his revenge....

*Look for the first book
in The Belles of Texas miniseries,
on sale in July wherever books are sold.*

HARLEQUIN *Super Romance*

COMING NEXT MONTH

Available July 14, 2009

WELCOME TO COWBOY COUNTRY

#1572 TEXAS WEDDING • Kathleen O'Brien

Just because Susannah Everly married Trent Maxwell doesn't mean she has to forgive him. They both know the deal with this union and it doesn't include rekindling their old love. But can she live a year with him and *not* give in to temptation?

#1573 NO HERO LIKE HIM • Elaine Grant
Hometown U.S.A.

Counting his life in eight-second increments is all Seth Morgan knows. Then a bull beats him up in the ring. Desperate to get his body back, he takes a job at a riding camp. All good until he falls for the boss, Claire Ford. Because he can't have her and the rodeo....

#1574 CAITLYN'S PRIZE • Linda Warren
The Belles of Texas

Thanks to her late father's gambling debts, Caitlyn Belle's High Five Ranch is in dire straits. If the ranch doesn't turn a profit in six months, it's to be sold to Judd Calhoun— the man she jilted years ago. And Cait knows Judd has been waiting for his revenge....

#1575 A RANCH CALLED HOME • Candy Halliday

Sara Watson will do anything to protect her son, Ben. So when Ben's uncle Gabe Coulter tracks them down, she can't resist his offer: a temporary marriage so Ben can know his heritage. Once she's at the ranch, it feels like the home she's always wanted.

#1576 COWBOY COMES BACK • Jeannie Watt
Going Back

Now that his rodeo career's kaput, Kade Danning has nowhere to go but home— if you can call it that. After hitting rock bottom, making amends is easy. But convincing Libby Hale to trust him again is harder than anything he's faced—in or out of the ring.

#1577 KIDS ON THE DOORSTEP • Kimberly Van Meter
Home in Emmett's Mill

John Murphy is a solitary man. Until he finds three abandoned little girls on his doorstep. He doesn't know anything about how to take care of kids! But he takes in the munchkins and vows to protect them—even if that means saving them from their own mother!